Part One

Winter 1976

MURDER AS USUAL

The newscaster gasped. "Mac Crenshaw has been shot by what appears to have been a woman in the crowd. Ladies and gentlemen, from here it seems she has blown off the top of Crenshaw's head. It is surely a ghastly assassination. There is no chance Crenshaw can have survived . . . Just beyond where he was standing when the shot was fired the killer has been thrown to the ground and someone in the Crenshaw group appears to be beating her—or him—with the butt end of a gun of some sort . . .

"Ladies and gentlemen, a local newsman has just informed me that the man who threw the killer to the ground was Mac Crenshaw's younger brother, William Crenshaw. And it was a woman! Yes, it was a woman, as yet unidentified. Oh, God, what a terrible, bloody climax to what started out to be a happy day!"

*Books you will enjoy
from Keyhole Crime:*

MURDER AS USUAL

Hugh Pentecost

KEYHOLE CRIME
London · Sydney

*First published in Great Britain 1978 by
Robert Hale Limited*

Copyright © 1977 by Judson Philips

Australian copyright 1981

Philippine copyright 1981

*This edition published 1981 by
Keyhole Crime, 15-16 Brook's Mews,
London W1A 1DR*

ISBN 0 263 73525 7

*Made and printed in Great Britain by
Cox & Wyman Ltd., Reading*

Contents

1

From the hillside, looking down on the snow-covered village, Cotter was reminded of a Grandma Moses painting. There were the distant church steeple, the red barns, the people looking tiny as they moved along the main street, the automobiles like toys. It was infinitely peaceful, bucolic, far removed from violence. Yet Cotter knew that somewhere along that main street there might still be a spot in the snow stained a bright scarlet by the blood of a man murdered by a psychotic assassin. The killer's blood might also be close by because she had been bludgeoned to death seconds after she had pulled the trigger that had snuffed out the life of a vital and vibrant man who might someday have been of enormous importance to the people of his country.

"He was going places," Senator Farraday had told Cotter. "All the way to the top, unless I miss my guess. What kind of a sick world are we living in, David?"

"A sick, sick world," David Cotter said.

"A world of guns, and bombs, and hijackers, kidnappers, and torturers," Farraday said. He had brought his fist down on his desk in the Senate Office Building in Washington. "I want the man behind that gun, David."

Cotter looked puzzled. "But the girl is dead, Senator."

"I said 'man' behind that gun," Farraday said. "The girl was a—a crazy, easily persuaded. Who persuaded her and why? Was it political? Was it personal? Was it revenge by some organized crime mob? I want answers, David."

"It's not exactly my line of work these days, Senator," Cotter said.

"You owe me, David," the Senator said. "I'm asking for payment."

Cotter, standing on that New England hillside, looking down at the village of Brownsville, turned to his car, prepared to drive down to the scene of an assassination. It was the beginning of his way of paying a debt to a friend.

He was named, rather absurdly for the time in which he lived and died, Marcus Aurelius after the Roman Emperor and stoic philosopher—Marcus Aurelius Crenshaw. It caused him quite a little trouble in his early school days. The jokes were endless. But later, when he became a national figure, first in the world of sports and then in politics, he was called by his initials, Mac. Mac Crenshaw was one of the few Ivy League football players to be a consensus All-American all over the country. Pro football scouts, owners, and coaches panted on his doorstep offering fabulous contracts. He could have been a millionaire in a very short time.

Mac Crenshaw wasn't tempted because he was already rich beyond accounting. The Crenshaw oil fortune. He had a Rhodes scholarship and he left the football world weeping while he headed for Oxford. Nor would he listen to offers two years later when he came back. Instead he went to law school and eventually, in his late twenties, he was admitted to the bar. Corporation law was his specialty and he, early on, demonstrated that he was brilliant at it. But neither the law nor even the Supreme Court were his goals.

Mac Crenshaw intended to become the President of the United States when the climate was right.

The idea of becoming President was not a childhood dream. It was a deliberate and carefully designed plan of Ross Crenshaw's. The oil tycoon, whose multinational corporate empire was bigger and more powerful than whole groups of nations, decided that his oldest son and heir should, by reason of his wealth and power, and by achieving the highest political office in the world, become the king of all he surveyed.

There were some lucky circumstances to implement the plan along the way, although Ross Crenshaw would not have considered them lucky. Of course his son would turn out to be handsome and magnetic. Weren't the Crenshaws old New England aristocrats, and wasn't Anne Crenshaw, his mother, an Elliot? Strong good looks were trademarks of both the Crenshaws and the Elliots. Charm was an inherited talent. It wasn't luck that Marcus—his father always called him Marcus—had athletic ability. All the Crenshaws were well coordinated. Mac Crenshaw's athletic career wasn't hurt by the fact that his father had heavy holdings in a chain of newspapers and a television network. But Mac would have made the headlines anyway, he was that good. Millions of people had seen his brilliant running and pass-catching on dozens of Saturday afternoons. They had seen his wide bright smile on television interviews and in magazine articles. Publicity searched him out, rather than his going after it.

Turning down million-dollar contracts with the football people made him something special. At Oxford he was still in the headlines while on his scholarship. He reached the quarter finals of the British Amateur Golf Championship. He won a downhill skiing championship at St. Moritz.

When he was in law school he married Gwendolyn Lassiter, a beautiful, dark-haired Boston socialite. She was Roger Lassiter's daughter, and the wedding at the Lassiter compound on

11

Cape Cod made a royal wedding look just a bit seedy.

Corporation law was a natural for Mac Crenshaw because he was the heir to the biggest of the big. While most people hear about it, they don't pay much attention to the fact that the big corporations run the world they live in.

A key part of Ross Crenshaw's plan was that Mac—or Marcus—would attach himself to some older man who was going places politically. The choice of that older man was of vital importance.

Another important necessity was a war record. "What did you do in the big war, Daddy?" was a question somebody who was going to be President had to be able to answer. Of course Mac Crenshaw was in a position to get just about what he wanted, so he enlisted in the Air Force, and was promptly attached to the Advocate General's staff. Mac Crenshaw wasn't a physical coward, but there was no sense in running the risk of a Vietcong sniper's bullet putting an end to Ross Crenshaw's master plan. But there was luck in terms of that plan. It fell to Mac Crenshaw to prosecute some black-market profiteering noncom officers in Saigon who had murdered some high-ranking Indochinese officials who got in their way. It was a scandalous case, and Mac Crenshaw, All-American golden boy, was in the headlines once more. He got a conviction and was nationally associated with "justice being done." As is not unusual in such cases, the men who were convicted and sentenced to death were small fry. The big shots who had gotten rich in the black market went fishing.

It wasn't too hard for Mac Crenshaw to leave the service when his time of enlistment was up. A special prosecutor in Washington, investigating corruption in high places in government, wanted the golden boy on his staff. How this special prosecutor got to know that he wanted Mac Crenshaw may just have had something to do with a suggestion from an important client of his in private practice who was president of a corporation which was a subsidiary of the Crenshaw empire.

Mac and Gwen Crenshaw bought a beautiful house in Virginia and were instantly in the social whirl in Washington. Working for the special prosecutor, Mac came into contact with Senator Lewis Farraday, chairman of a Senate subcommittee listening to the special prosecutor and his staff. Some of the hearings were on television and Farraday, not too well known outside his own state, was suddenly a public figure of consequence. Farraday was a tough, craggy, apparently rockhonest man with a keen wit and rapier kills when dealing with evasive witnesses. People began to whisper about Lewis Farraday as a possible candidate for the Presidency. The out-party needed a man the whole country would recognize.

One night, in his Virginia home, Mac Crenshaw was called away from a gay party to find his father waiting for him in the library.

"We are going to support Farraday for the Party's nomination at next summer's convention," Ross Crenshaw told his son. "I think he's the man we've been waiting for, Marcus, win or lose. I suggest you take a leave of absence from your job and offer your services to Farraday."

"If he'll have me," Mac Crenshaw said.

"Oh, he'll have you," the elder Crenshaw said, his smile a tight-lipped imitation. "You'll work for him in the primaries. I believe there are a couple of dozen important ones. You will make contacts, friends, all across the country."

"For Farraday."

"For yourself, you idiot," Ross Crenshaw said. "Eight years from now you will be making the run on your own. This is groundwork for you. The first two primaries are in New England, your own bailiwick. You'll get your feet wet where you've already got friends."

And so it was that Ross Crenshaw sent his golden son to his death, where he had friends—and at least one mortal enemy.

13

Jack Murphy was in his seventies, a trim, white-haired little Irishman—his hair had been white since he was thirty-five—with bristling black eyebrows and bright blue eyes alive with perpetual humor. His complexion was ruddy, and anyone with an eye for it knew that Jack Murphy had drunk a lot of good whiskey in his time and enjoyed every drop of it. It explained why he had lost so many good newspaper jobs over the years. Managing editors put up with him beyond the break-point of endurance because he was a brilliant investigative reporter and also a colorful writer—a rare combination. But always, in the end, too many deadlines were missed. Long periods of routine drinking were always climaxed by a colossal bender. Murphy would disappear for a couple of weeks and reappear, shaky, eyes bloodshot, with his hand raised in a solemn oath. No more drinking, ever! He always kept the pledge until the next payday.

Jack Murphy was working on what could well be his last job. The *Capital Courier*, the only daily newspaper in the primary State, was owned and edited by one Lester Owen, who had made a national reputation for himself as a political giant killer. Many promising careers had been blasted in the primaries in Owen's state. Les Owen was a hatchet man who enjoyed the taste of the blood he drew.

It appeared to be an accident that Lester Owen, on a visit to Boston at Christmastime, ran into Jack Murphy in a bar that was a cheerful hangout for ward politicians in the city. Once, twenty years ago, Jack Murphy had worked for a brief spell on the *Capitol Courier*, and lost the job for the usual reasons. There was a slight variation to the usual firing. Lester Owen, a giant of a man with curly red hair and a knife-slit of a mouth, who had developed his muscles as a young man in the logging business during cold New England winters, took the time to throw Murphy bodily out onto the street.

"Don't ever show your face in this town again, you Irish

14

bastard," Owen bellowed, "or I'll personally throw you into the town sewer!"

Now, twenty years later, Lester Owen walked up to Jack Murphy in Cassiday's Bar and Grill in Boston, patted Murphy on the shoulder, and said: "Long time no see, Jack-boy!"

And Murphy, laughter in his blue eyes, knew it wasn't an accidental meeting. Lester Owen never forgave anybody unless it was to his advantage.

"Buy you a whiskey, Jack?" Owen invited.

Accident my foot, Murphy thought. It was against his policy ever to refuse a drink. They stood at Cassiday's bar, each with a foot on the brass rail. Jack Daniel's was ordered, more expensive than the regular bar whiskey.

"You working?" Owen asked. He knew the answer, of course.

"I am, as my actor friends say," Murphy said, " 'at leisure.' " Probably actors hadn't said that for fifty years, but no matter.

"Interested in a single assignment?"

"For money," Murphy said. He took a swallow of his whiskey and smiled at Owen. "You picked out your whipping boy for the primaries, Lester?"

Nobody called Owen by his first name unless he was a close, close friend—or a victim. When Owen didn't react, Murphy knew he was about to be conned.

"I sure don't want to see Senator Farraday come out on top of the heap," Owen said.

"Tough guy to clobber if he has his heart set on it," Murphy said. "Those TV hearings have made him a kind of a hero to some people. What have you got on him?"

Owen made a growling sound in his throat and gestured to the bartender for refills. "If I had enough on him, I wouldn't be talking to you about a job, Jack-boy."

Murphy made sure there wasn't a drop left in his glass before the bartender took it away to fill it. "You must want him real

15

bad, Lester," Murphy said, "or you'd pick on someone else. I've been listening around and I hear the Crenshaw people are backing him. Going up against them is looking for man-sized trouble."

"Self-righteous bastard!" Owen said.

"Crenshaw?"

"Farraday!"

It began to filter through to Murphy. The junior Senator from Owen's state, a year ago, had appeared before Farraday's committee and later the special prosecutor had got him on charges of bribery and other financial skulduggery. Senator Martin Cleary had managed to stall off a jail sentence so far, appeal, and finally the big one to the Supreme Court probably months away. But he hadn't been able to run for reelection. The cloud was too dark. Martin Cleary had been Owen's fair-haired boy. Farraday had done him in, with the help of the special prosecutor and his young assistant, Mac Crenshaw. Revenge was the name of the game.

Murphy looked longingly at his second drink. He wanted it, but maybe he'd better pass it up. He didn't think he wanted to get caught in the Crenshaw meat grinder.

Owen looked at Murphy, his eyes narrowed, his smile that knife-blade slit. "You may be a drunk, Jack-boy," he said, "but you've always been able to add up two and two."

"And make it come out five," Murphy said. He sighed and reached for his glass. What the hell? One meat grinder or another was going to get him sooner or later. "Just what do you want of me, Lester? Surely not to write your editorials."

"Farraday's advance army is moving into my territory in a couple of weeks," Owen said. "Farraday himself won't show till the very last moment; a day or two before the primary. He will stay on his job, which is mugging in front of the TV cameras in Washington. But his golden boy, the famous Mac Crenshaw, is coming in ahead of him. The charmer! The Frank

Merriwell hero of most of the people in my state."

"He cost me money once," Murphy said. He was looking well back. "Three touchdowns in the Bowl against Yale. I'd bet my shirt on Yale that Saturday."

"He knifed my friend Martin Cleary in the back!" Owen said. He was talking about the man's world, not the kid stuff of college football. But there was no denying football made Mac Crenshaw a dangerous campaigner. That's how much sense the voters made.

"Just what do you want of me, Lester?" Murphy asked.

"I want to nail Crenshaw before Farraday ever appears on the scene," Owen said. "Look at him, Murphy. A sports hero, a war hero, a society glamor boy with a beautiful wife. Everyone admires him, but deep down everyone hates him, envies him. If we could get something on him, some morals charge, Jackboy, the voters would go righteous on him and attack him like a pack of wild dogs. Farraday would be a dead duck before he ever got here."

It was an old pattern, Murphy knew. Prove that Mac Crenshaw was in the wrong bed, or that his gorgeous wife was in the wrong bed, and he was done for, and Farraday was gone with him.

"There have been whispers," Owen said, not as though he believed it, "that Mac Crenshaw may be a queer."

"Baloney!" Murphy said.

"A lot of athletes and soldiers are queer," Owen said.

"Double baloney."

"They still don't like adulterers in my state," Owen said. "Half the women in Washington are after young Crenshaw, I hear. He has to be screwing someone besides that doll he's married to."

"And you want me to park under his bed," Murphy said. He looked like a man who had just tasted something bad.

"Get something I can use on him, Murphy, and there'll be

enough money to keep you in booze the rest of your natural life."

"I'm not going to frame him or anyone else, Lester," Murphy said. "I'll go after facts for you, but they have to be real facts, true facts."

"Fine," Owen said. He brought his fist down on the bar. "There *has* to be something we can use. There always is if you dig deep enough."

Murphy thought he remembered that it was Mark Twain who had said that the trouble with being a liar is that you can't believe what anyone else tells you. The trouble with Lester Owen was that, being a monster, he assumed that everyone else was a monster "if you could dig deep enough." Being a winning monster was Lester's game.

"Why me?" Murphy asked. "Why did you come looking for me, Lester?"

Owen laughed and signaled to the bartender for a third round. He'd got what he'd come after. "Everyone knows that I kicked you out of the *Courier* office with my own right foot, Jack-boy. They'd know you're the last person I'd hire for anything, and they probably think I'm the last person you'd work for. They don't know the depths of your thirst, Jack-boy."

"You sonofabitch," Murphy said quietly.

Owen laughed. Name-calling didn't matter when you had what you wanted. He mentioned sums of money, and Murphy listened, staring into the amber-colored liquor in his glass. He had a feeling the sauce would be the death of him.

And that was how it happened that Jack Murphy was standing not ten feet away from Mac Crenshaw when the gun was fired and the golden boy's brains and blood were spattered onto a New England snowdrift.

It wasn't difficult to get a picture of exactly what happened that day. Literally a picture. There had been TV cameras at

18

the Brownsville airport where Mac Crenshaw and his entourage arrived in a chartered plane. There had been TV cameras along the motor route to the Rotary luncheon where Mac Crenshaw had been guest of honor and made a warm and amusing speech. There had been TV cameras covering Mac Crenshaw's walk along Brownsville's main street, shaking hands with hundreds of eager greeters on his way to be guest of honor at the Olympic Ski Jumping Trials on the outskirts of town. A skiing champion himself, Mac Crenshaw was an ideal person to hand out the trophies to the lucky winners.

He never got to give out the trophies. He never even got to the trials.

Films of an event that TV news people are prepared to cover are usually expert as to detail. But David Cotter knew that when the unexpected occurs there's apt to be a gap in the camera record, a moment of confusion, in which it's obvious the cameraman has been frozen for an instant, and then uncertain what he should be covering, hoping that someone else on another camera would catch what he was missing. So it was that the precise moment of Mac Crenshaw's assassination was incomplete on film. One camera was focused on Crenshaw's smiling face, as he shook hands, sometimes reaching to a rear row of spectators as if he saw someone he knew. It suddenly looked as though someone had poured acid on the film, because the smiling face dissolved in a scarlet fog. Behind it was the sound of the gun and the shocked voice of the TV reporter saying "Oh, Jesus!"

The second camera had been on the crowd, tightly lined along the Main Street sidewalk, all smiling, all eager to greet the conquering hero. By sheer bad luck, from the cameraman's point of view, they hadn't been focused on the girl. There was the sound of the shot, the announcer's startled and shocked profanity, the camera's searching to find the action, and then the announcer's cold and professional voice.

"Mac Crenshaw has been shot by what appears to have been a woman in the crowd. Ladies and gentlemen, from here it seems she has blown off the top of Crenshaw's head. It is surely a ghastly assassination. There is no chance Crenshaw can have survived. . . . Just beyond where he was standing when the shot was fired the killer has been thrown to the ground and someone in the Crenshaw group appears to be beating her—or him— with the butt end of a gun of some sort. . . . The Crenshaw man is being pulled away from the killer now. If I seem uncertain about the sex of the killer, it's because she—or he—is wearing ski clothes: ski pants, a fur jacket, a knitted toque pulled down over long blond hair. It could be a man or a woman, but I heard her scream just before she was thrown down by— Who did you say?— Ladies and gentleman, a local newsman has just informed me that the man who threw the killer to the ground was Mac Crenshaw's younger brother, William Crenshaw. And it was a woman! Yes, it was a woman, as yet unidentified. Oh, God, what a terrible, bloody climax to what started out to be a happy day!"

It was two days after the event that David Cotter saw the films, courtesy of the local State Police. The girl assassin was still not identified. Captain Shane; locally in charge, looked like what he was, a man who hadn't slept for two nights. His skin was drawn tight over the bones of his face and looked like faded parchment.

"According to the medical examiner she was probably eighteen, nineteen years old. No one locally could identify her," Shane told Cotter. "A man who runs a lunchroom down Main Street says the girl was there before Crenshaw's plane arrived. She had coffee and Danish. He remembers her because she was carrying a muff made of the same fur as her jacket. You don't see muffs every day, which is why this restaurant man recalls her. She was alone."

"Fingerprints?" Cotter asked.

"We have nothing on record that matches," Shane said. "So far the FBI in Washington has drawn a blank."

"William Crenshaw actually killed her?"

Shane nodded. "He was just a step behind his brother. They were inching along as Mac Crenshaw shook hands with each person in line. He was smiling, kind of a fixed smile, I imagine. But the people were all smiling back and cheering him, all quite genuine. This girl took her hand out of the muff she was carrying and extended it toward Mac Crenshaw. It wasn't until he reached out to take it that he saw that it held a gun. Bill Crenshaw saw it at the same moment and made a dive for her, but too late. She fired, and she was screaming something crazy. 'You must stop poisoning the world!' A number of people were sure she said just that. Bill Crenshaw hit her with a flying tackle, and, of course, he grappled for the gun. When he got it, he turned to look at his brother and saw the horrible remains of a face. Instinctively, in grief and rage, he began beating at the girl's head with the butt of her own gun. Before he could be pulled away he had crushed her skull to a bloody pulp."

"Charges against him?" Cotter asked.

"God, no!" Shane said. "What would you have done, Mr. Cotter?"

Jack Murphy was on the second day of building the colossal bender of all time. He was doing it in public, not his usual pattern. Some bartenders wouldn't have served him, particularly on the second day, but Warren Hunter, proprietor of Hunter's Lodge, was an old friend, and he knew very well that Jack Murphy never made trouble. He just got slowly blind, but it took him a long time to get there. On the afternoon of the assassination, Murphy, cold sober, had walked into the lodge, cornered his old friend Warren Hunter, and handed him two hundred dollars in cash.

"I am going to tie one on," Murphy said. "Keep pouring till you run out of money."

Hunter didn't ask why. The whole town of Brownsville was in shock. He noticed that Murphy kept brushing at something invisible on his coat.

"I was no farther away from him than I am from you," Murphy said, talking to his friend across the bar. "I keep thinking some of his brains may have spattered on me." He shuddered. "I'll start with a double, friend."

The lodge stayed crowded that afternoon and night. Nobody talked about anything but the tragedy. Everybody was certain that in the next moment, the next hour, the State Police or the FBI would identify the girl who had murdered Mac Crenshaw. It didn't happen. The reason, they all knew, was that there was no picture of the girl to circulate. Bill Crenshaw's savage attack on her had obliterated her face. The police artist had tried to draw a likeness from the lunchroom man's description of her.

He was the only person in town who admitted to having seen her. But his description of her and the police drawing produced no results. No one admitted knowing her from the drawing, which was reproduced in newspapers all across the country.

At the end of that first night Warren Hunter, after his bar closed, bedded Jack Murphy down in an upstairs room. Murphy took a bottle of bourbon with him, and when Hunter looked in on him the next morning, the bottle was empty.

When the bar opened the second day, Murphy appeared, shaven, respectable, but walking a little like a man on a tightrope. He had hoped that the first day's onslaught on the sauce would wipe out the pain that was eating at his gut. Murphy's problem was that he had convinced himself that he was an accessory to a murder. It never occurred to him, from the moment the girl fired her gun and he'd seen the horrible obliteration of Mac Crenshaw's handsome face, that Lester Owen wasn't behind what had happened. He, Murphy, had sold himself to Owen, so he, morally, was just as guilty as Owen, who had almost certainly planned it all. Worse than that, he didn't have the guts to speak out, to tell what he knew, what he had been hired to do. His job had been to hunt for skeletons in the Crenshaw closet. That wasn't a crime, but his mind, ice-cold and untouched by a staggering amount of booze, told him he was part of a conspiracy that had led to murder. Murphy didn't want to spend the rest of his life in jail, or find himself hanging from some farmer's apple tree, strung up there by an angry lynch mob. He was a coward, and he was going to have to live with a strangling guilt for whatever time he had left.

On the second day the assassination was still the only topic of conversation in Brownsville. The picture hadn't identified the girl, but what about the gun she'd used? It was a .45 army issue, the serial number carefully filed away. Ballistics had fired test bullets from it and the results were sent on to the FBI in

23

Washington in the hope there'd be some record of its having been used before. So far, nothing.

In the early afternoon of the second day a stranger came into Hunter's Lodge, took a stool at the bar, and ordered a corned beef sandwich on rye and a bottle of ale. He was right next to Murphy, who was still trying to blot out the world with double bourbons. The stranger had a copy of that day's *Capitol Courier* and he opened it up on the bar. A black headline screamed a message.

COURIER OFFERS $10,000 FOR INFORMATION
THAT WILL IDENTIFY CRENSHAW KILLER

Murphy saw it and he laughed, a harsh, bitter laugh.

The stranger looked at him. The stranger was a nice-looking young man, Murphy thought. Probably about forty, which was young to Jack Murphy in his seventies. Looked a little like Burt Lancaster, the actor. He was a man about six feet tall, well-muscled, in very good shape for his age. His hair was a sandy brown, curly, his eyes a mild blue—mild, yet somehow Murphy had the idea that the stranger could read the shirt label on the inside of his collar if he chose. Those eyes were amused at the moment, as though the stranger hoped Murphy would share the joke with him. He wore gray slacks and what must have been an expensive brown tweed jacket which now had leather patches at the elbows. Navy-blue sports shirt. He had hung a fleece-lined overcoat and a blue ski cap on the hooks beside the bar. Strangers attracted attention under normal conditions in Brownsville. On this day the conditions weren't normal, the place flooded with strangers.

"That's the first time I've heard anyone laugh in this town today," the stranger said. His voice was pleasant, friendly.

Murphy felt his heart pound against his ribs. Maybe this was the time to clear his conscience, tell all. It would be committing suicide, but that could be better than living with his guilt.

He pointed an unsteady finger at the *Courier's* headline.

"Joke of the year," he said.

"Oh?" The stranger's sandy eyebrows rose.

"You ever hear of Les Owen who owns and edits that rag?" Murphy asked.

"New England's political hatchet man," the stranger said, smiling.

"He wanted to get Crenshaw in order to get Senator Farraday," Murphy said. "I know, because he hired me to help him. Now he covers himself by offering a reward. That's the joke, Mister—"

"Cotter," the stranger said. "As a matter of fact I'm a friend of Senator Farraday's, which is why I'm here in town. You think Owen is involved in Crenshaw's death?"

"Who else?" Murphy asked. His voice was unsteady now, shaken. "Crenshaw was a local hero. All-American football star, decorated war veteran, television star, you might say, from the hearings in Washington. He could win the primary for Farraday without the Senator ever coming here. Crenshaw had to be stopped. And I—well, I was part of a conspiracy to stop him."

"Did you get something on Crenshaw?" Cotter asked.

"No. Which is why Owen had to go to extremes to stop him."

Cotter looked at the sandwich and the bottle of ale the bartender brought him, but he made no move toward them. He was frowning slightly.

"I don't think I buy that," he said.

"But I tell you—!"

"I don't think you've thought it through," Cotter said. "A scandal involving Crenshaw would have hurt the Senator, perhaps badly. But Crenshaw murdered on television, with the whole country seeing it on their home screens, just about guarantees the Senator a landslide victory in the primary. Mur-

25

dering Crenshaw is the last thing in the world Owen would be involved in. He's lost his war before it really started." He gave Murphy a gentle smile. "I think you can let your conscience rest, Mr. Murphy."

Murphy didn't stop to think that he'd never mentioned his name to Cotter. The room began to spin around him. Then he toppled off his bar stool and fell flat on his face on the floor.

The bartender came quickly around to him. "Been waiting for that to happen for the last twenty-four hours," he said. "Poor old bastard must have drunk a half a barrel of whiskey since yesterday. He sure can pour it on. I wouldn't want to have his hangover."

Cotter smiled. "As a matter of fact I think he'll feel marvelous when he comes to," he said.

Marvelous and ready to help, Cotter thought.

The debt that David Cotter owed to Senator Farraday was one of the most elementary man-to-man obligations. In 1951 General Farraday, head of Army Intelligence in Korea, had saved the life of nineteen-year-old Private David Cotter, the general's jeep driver. The jeep had hit a land mine. The general had been thrown clear but the young Private Cotter was pinned in the wreckage, badly hurt, about to be burned alive. The general, ignoring sniper bullets, turning away from his own chance to escape, had pulled Cotter out of the wreckage. They would almost certainly have been riddled by the snipers but for the lucky arrival of an army helicopter, attracted by the explosion of the jeep, which proceeded to bomb the snipers out of the area. Under that cover the general had hoisted the unconscious Cotter onto his back and carried him through the jungle to safety. It was gallantry beyond the call of duty for the head of Army Intelligence in Korea. Cotter was just a number, an expendable number.

There's a curious drawing together of men in such a situation. One is forever in debt to the other for saving him. But the hero is equally bound, subconsciously grateful for having been given the opportunity to be a hero. And General Farraday was a decent man, which helped things along. He followed Cotter's recovery, visiting him almost every day in the hospital. Young Cotter was properly respectful, expressed his genuine feeling of obligation, but without fawning. Farraday, a bachelor, felt he had acquired a son. Cotter, much younger and less experienced, was probably more realistic. He felt that he had acquired a friend.

During his period of recuperation Cotter found himself attached to Farraday's staff in a clerical capacity. He learned a good deal about intelligence work. When the war ended and the general and the private returned home, the relationship continued. Cotter had no family and he found himself living in the general's home. Farraday insisted that Cotter complete his education. Cotter, who had been drafted into the army after his freshman year in college, was able to get his degree in a speeded-up two years, working in vacation times for Farraday. The general now had turned to politics, and in the same year that Cotter got his degree, Lewis Farraday was elected to the United States Senate.

Senator Farraday's prime concern, politically, was the growth and power of the great multinational corporations. Cotter found himself in charge of a small staff of investigators for the Senator. After a number of years Cotter set himself up in business. It might have been called Industrial Espionage. The name on the office door was DAVID COTTER ASSOCIATES. It was a profitable business. From time to time Cotter was able to pass on important information to his benefactor. On several occasions he had taken on a full-scale investigation for Farraday. Socially the two men stayed close to each other, almost the father-and-son relationship Farraday felt.

There was one gap in that friendship, a natural one. Shortly

27

after Cotter had moved out on his own he fell in love with a beautiful and charming girl and married her. He discovered a happiness he didn't dream could exist. It ended tragically. A little more than a year after their wedding Marjorie Cotter died, agonizingly, of an inoperable intestinal cancer. It cut off a whole phase of Cotter's life. Cut it off forever, Cotter thought. From then on he would be without love, without anyone to share with.

"Marjorie would want you to find another woman," Farraday told him.

"No chance," Cotter said, his pain so deep. "Not ever."

Life went on, Cotter working long hours every day. As each day drew to an end, he was filled with dread. He would sleep in a bed somewhere—"somewhere" because he had sold the home he'd bought for himself and Marjorie. He lived in hotels, moving periodically because each place he lived was suddenly clouded by pain. He would fight sleep, but in the end sheer physical fatigue made it a losing battle. Then, in the first phase of drifting off, he would reach out for someone who wasn't there, who would never be there again. He would spring awake, sitting up in his bed, sweating. If he had been willing to admit it, he could have told you there were tears. After that he would sleep, slugged out, drugged by pain.

After some weeks he would move to a new hotel, a new place, hoping that the nightmare would be left behind him. It had never quite happened, although the acute symptoms were less severe, chiefly because he disciplined his memory not to remember—too much.

It had been almost twenty-five years to the day since General Farraday had rescued Private Cotter from a burning jeep in Korea, that the general, now Senator, had asked for payment.

"I want the man behind the gun, David."

Cotter never thought for a moment of saying "no." He owed.

* * *

28

Cotter knew hatred when he saw it. Lester Owen, sitting across a cluttered desk from him in the *Courier* office, hated him, even though they had never laid eyes on each other before this meeting. It occurred to Cotter that Owen wasn't capable of any emotion but hatred. He hated you, more or less, but liked no one.

"How come the Senator hasn't offered a reward?" Owen asked in his rasping voice.

Cotter gave the man his gentle smile. "He hired me instead."

Owen made a snorting sound. "You are supposed to be smarter than the State Police, the FBI, probably the CIA? What crap!"

Cotter's smile widened. "I'm supposed to have a private radar system that will tell me where to start looking," he said.

"Farraday is a goddam dreamer!" Owen said. "Private radar system! That self-righteous sonofabitch thinks God is on his side. I'll tell you something, Cotter. Lewis Farraday has no more chance of getting his party's nomination at the convention in July than I have."

"A little better chance than you have," Cotter said, "because you have no chance at all. And the Senator will win the primary here by a landslide after what happened to Crenshaw. That was bad luck for you, wasn't it?"

"Incredible piece of luck for the Senator!"

Cotter took a pipe from his pocket and began to fill it from an oilskin pouch. "My problem is to find out where to start looking," he said. "That's where that private radar system comes in. For example, a very drunken, very conscience-stricken little man told me I should start here."

"Jack Murphy, that Irish bastard!"

Cotter held a lighter to his pipe, and when it was going well: "That's where my private radar system comes in, Owen. I explained to Murphy, carefully, that assassinating Crenshaw was the last thing in the world you wanted. It insured a whopping victory for the Senator."

"And what did Jack-boy have to say to that?"

"He passed out cold. He was so happy at being convinced he wasn't an accessory to a murder."

"Sniveling little creep!"

"Aren't you going to ask me why I'm here, since you know now I don't suspect you?" Cotter was still smiling.

"So why are you here, Mr. Bones?"

"Because I want help from you."

Owen laughed a deep rumbling laugh. "*You* want help from *me?*"

"Want it and am going to get it," Cotter said, and suddenly the mild blue eyes were not so mild.

"I wouldn't piss on Farraday or his people if they were on fire," Owen said.

"But you would piss on yourself if you were on fire, wouldn't you, Owen? Because I want to tell you, you are on fire, burning bright."

"What the hell are you talking about?"

"I never confront an armed man without being armed myself," Cotter said.

"You're armed? With what?" Owen's eyes were narrowed and a muscle rippled along the line of his jaw.

"The Senator isn't a fool," Cotter said. "Whatever else you may think of him, you'll have to concede he's a skillful politician. He's known for months he was going to have to fight you here in the primaries. So he was ready."

"With what?"

"The secret history of the life of Lester Owen," Cotter said. Strong white teeth were clamped over the stem of his pipe as he started to count off on his fingers. "Illegal contributions to a recent Presidential campaign. Using the *Courier* to discredit a young county attorney who was about to nail your friend, the

30

governor of this great State, for being a pawn of the gambling interests that really control the State's finances." Cotter looked up. "I use the phrase 'friend of yours' in the most casual sort of way, Owen. You don't have friends. You only have people you've got something on, like the governor."

Owen shook his head. "If that's what you call being armed, Cotter, I have to tell you all you've got is a toy cap pistol. I've paid my fine for making an illegal contribution. That's water over the dam. I defended the governor because I know he's innocent. There's nothing private about either of those things. Armed, my foot!"

Cotter leaned back in his chair, his eyes raised toward the ceiling, as if he saw visions there. "There is a young man who once worked on the *Courier* as a reporter. His name is Paul Wilson. He wrote a book about you."

"Scurrilous and libelous," Owen said. "He couldn't get a publisher for it. A vicious little twerp who thought he could make a fast buck by defaming me. No reputable publisher would touch it because they all knew I'd sue them out of their britches."

"He hasn't gotten himself a publisher yet," Cotter said, "but he got one very interested reader, Senator Farraday. The Senator put some professional investigators on it, tracking down each individual accusation in Wilson's book. I won't go over them all. But there is one that fascinates me. Wilson claims that you are a sexual sadist. He says there are a long list of women in this State who were forced to give in to you because of threats against their husbands or fathers or brothers. You like forcing yourself on women who don't want you. That's your particular perversion."

"What crap!" Owen said.

"There was a Brownsville housewife whose husband got into some kind of trouble. You got the word to the husband that unless his wife would submit to a night in your bed he would

31

spend the next fifteen years in jail. The wife agreed, or at least she said she agreed. On her way to an assignation with you at whatever place you use for these adventures, the lady jumped off the bridge over the Wattamasic River and was drowned."

Owen shook his head again, but this time it was a little like a punch-drunk fighter. "That was Ella Marston," he said. His speech sounded a little thick. "But the rest of it is pure nonsense. The Marstons were my friends. Fred Marston has a very good job in the State Capitol."

"Which you got for him."

"Sure I got it for him. Ella's suicide was a tragedy for Fred. He couldn't bear to go on living here in Brownsville. People blamed him for Ella's jumping in the river. Husbands are always blamed when a wife goes haywire."

"And in this case rightly so," Cotter said. He sounded, suddenly, very cold and hard. "He asked her to submit to you to save his hide."

"That is absolutely crazy," Owen said.

"Not absolutely," Cotter said. "Ella Marston loved her husband. She agreed to do what he asked. But she knew she just couldn't go through with it. And so she wrote a letter to a friend."

Owen sat straight up in his chair. "What friend?"

"Oh, I wouldn't dream of telling you that, Owen. The friend would probably have an accident. But I hasten to say that would be useless. The friend no longer has the letter. It's in safe hands, ready to be used when necessary."

"I don't believe a word of it," Owen said. "I don't believe there's a friend or a letter. Ella Marston died two years ago. Why didn't the friend use the letter?"

"Ella Marston agreed to save her husband by submitting to you, Owen. She couldn't go through with it, but she decided to save him anyway. As long as her husband was safe and gainfully employed, the friend was instructed to keep the letter private. If anything went wrong with her husband's career, the friend was instructed to turn over the letter to the proper authorities. That letter is Fred Marston's insurance policy." Cotter's smile, cold now, reappeared. "You see, I am armed."

Little beads of sweat had appeared across Owen's forehead. "You're trying to blackmail me," he said.

"Dog eat dog," Cotter said.

Owen drew a deep breath. "What do you want of me?"

"I told you, help."

"What kind of help? Not a word of this story of yours is true, but if that crazy woman wrote such a letter, it could be big trouble."

"You wanted to discredit Mac Crenshaw," Cotter said. "You hired Jack Murphy to help you. But I can't believe he's the only person you hired. I want to know what you found, what you had. I want to know where to start looking for the girl who killed Crenshaw. I want to know who got her twisted mind to work for him. I want to find the man behind her gun. The primary here made a perfect cover for the truth. Was it a family problem? Was it a political problem? Was it someone who was going to be in trouble before the Senate Committee? You have dirtier sources of information than I have. I want your help."

"I haven't any kind of lead!" Owen insisted. "The girl was one of those crazy modern revolutionaries. 'You must stop poisoning the world!' she was screaming when Crenshaw's brother killed her. A nut, like one of those Manson kids."

Cotter tapped out his pipe in an ash tray by his chair and stood up. "I'll give you twenty-four hours to come up with something useful, Owen," he said. "After that I begin unveiling the true story of Lester Owen's sex life."

Owen sat slumped in his chair. "I'll do what I can," he muttered.

Cotter walked out into the bright, cold winter day. He felt

33

just a little ashamed of himself. The story of Ella Marston's suicide and the reason for it were in Paul Wilson's unpublished book. But there was no courtroom proof. The friend and the letter were simple inventions of Cotter's. You had to fight a monster monstrously, he told himself.

The girl—Cotter thought of her as a girl—was probably in her early thirties. Cotter had trained himself to apply specifics to people. Later descriptions, if needed, should be accurate. About five feet six, a hundred and fifteen pounds; coppery red hair, worn shoulder length, good figure, gray-green eyes. She dressed simply—but not inexpensively. On the desk in her office was a little brass plaque that read MS BRANSON. Cotter was all for equal rights, but it irritated him slightly not to know from the Ms whether the woman he was talking to was single or married.

"I'm sorry to barge in on you at a time that must be most difficult for you, Miss Branson," Cotter said. Let her correct him if it should be Mrs. Branson.

"One has to go on functioning," she said. "Senator Farrady asked me to be as cooperative as I can. I suppose no one wants answers to this tragedy more than I. But I don't know how I can help you, Mr. Cotter."

Cotter looked out the office window toward the dome of the Capitol. The snow-banked New England countryside he'd left a few hours ago had seemed defiantly cheerful despite the background of horror. Washington was bleak, windy and cold.

Cotter had gone straight from the airport to Senator Far-raday's office. Unless the girl who had shot Crenshaw was identified, it could be a long haul to get to the truth.

"The State Police and the FBI are much better equipped to make that identification than I am," Cotter told his friend. "I picked up a friend in Brownsville who'll be working for me there. Old-time newspaperman named Murphy."

34

Farraday smiled. "Jack Murphy? I know him. He used to cover the Washington beat for one of the press associations. Good man when he was sober. He must be getting on."

"Middle seventies, I'd guess, but very chipper when he's sober. He wants to help. At least he'll be a listening post in Brownsville. My problem is to know where to start here, Senator." Cotter paused. "There's the special prosecutor's office. Was Crenshaw about to set off a charge under someone? Could it be some enemy of his father's? Ross Crenshaw has a world full of enemies. I don't mind telling you I think the old man was using you to promote Mac's future."

"I haven't a doubt of it," Farraday said. His deeply lined face was set hard. "But why not? I think Mac could have gone to the very top. By the time he was ready to take aim at the White House, I'd be writing my memoirs. I was willing to be used, David."

"Somebody else who could look into the future may have decided this was the time to put an end to the Crenshaw dream," Cotter said.

"Find him for me," Farraday said, his voice harsh.

"On the other hand," Cotter said, "it could be something quite personal and intimate; someone using the political situation as a screen, a cover."

Farraday was silent for a moment, staring down at the papers on his desk without seeing them. "If I were going to write a biography of Mac Crenshaw," he said finally, "the person I'd go to first is Margaret Branson."

"Who is she?"

"His secretary. Very confidential secretary. Executive type. I've heard him say he couldn't get along without Maggie. Attractive woman who knows every twist and turn of his legal career, kept his social schedule in order. 'Even picks my neckties for me,' Mac once told me. 'Not what she thinks looks well on me, but what she thinks someone else will think looks well.

The first thing anyone notices about a man is his necktie.' "

"Or in this day and age the fact that he isn't wearing one," Cotter said.

"Maggie can tell you everything there is to know about Mac —if she will," Farraday said.

"She's in her early thirties now," Farraday said. "She's worked for Mac for almost ten years. She's vulnerable in just one area. Like so many women in her position, she is—was— totally and hopelessly in love with the boss. She won t tell you anything she thinks he wouldn't want you to know. But she wants his killer caught just as badly as we do. Unless—"

"Unless what?"

"Unless it would reveal something about Mac she intends to keep secret forever. But she's a starting point, David. I'll call her and say nice things about you."

Looking at Maggie Branson, sitting behind her desk, Cotter thought there must be a man in her life. This was too much woman to have spent ten years making doe's eyes at another woman's husband.

"The Senator says I am to trust you, Mr. Cotter," she said. The voice was cool and controlled. He guessed Wellesley or Smith. It turned out, at some later time, to have been Smith.

Cotter smiled at her. "So how much you trust me depends on how much you trust the Senator," he said. The smile vanished. "I hate pawing around in a dead man's affairs, Miss Branson. But it may be essential in order to find a starting point. Senator Farraday hopes you and Mac's family may be more willing to talk to me, one man, who is advertised as being discreet and on your side, rather than to an impersonal police force, a government bureau, even the special prosecutor. I have no reason to want to leak any sort of personal information about Mac. But the more I can get to know about him, the better chance I have of getting pointed in the right direction."

"To do what? To find what?" she asked.

"My assignment from the Senator is to find the man behind the gun."

"He doesn't believe it was just some drug-crazed young fanatic?"

"He doesn't, and I don't," Cotter said.

"And I don't," she said, after a moment of silence.

He waited for her to go on. He sensed that she was trying to make up her mind about him. Which doors should she open, and which keep closed?

"The logical place to begin would seem to be his job with the special prosecutor. He was into people's lives, careers, undercover maneuverings. There are people in high places who would go to almost any lengths to avoid exposure."

"As far as murder?" she asked.

"As far as murder," Cotter said. "The clever ones manage it in clever ways. A hit-and-run driver, a poison-induced heart attack, or the new patterns of a bomb in a public place that kills a dozen people including the target. Political assassinations are part of our life today. There were the Kennedys, both shot down by some kind of psychotic; Martin Luther King, ditto; George Wallace, again by a freak of some sort; the attempts on President Ford's life by whacked-out women. We always come up with the obvious killer, and yet we can never be totally convinced it wasn't a larger conspiracy with others involved who never come to the surface. What happened to Mac Crenshaw is in the classic mold. What did you call her, a drug-crazed young fanatic? Well, the Senator believes, and I agree, that the nameless girl in New England is just a pawn in a very complex game."

Margaret Branson let out her breath in a long sigh. "I'm glad somebody has finally said it."

"You have a theory?"

"No. Not yet, anyway." She gave Cotter a long steady look. "I'm snowed under here, David. Loose ends. Papers, documents, files that all have to be sorted out and delivered to the proper people. A lot of this has to be done yesterday. If we're to talk long enough to make any sense, it's going to have to be later today—tonight. Dinner?"

"Fine," Cotter said.

"My place," she said. "I have a lot of material there."

"I don't want to impose," he said.

"Look, David, if we're going to go into this thing, let's not be formal about it. There's a lot to talk about and we'd better find a place where we won't be interrupted. Your place, if you'd prefer it."

"I don't really have what you'd call a 'place,' " he said. "I'm a hotel hopper."

"Then my place," she said. She scribbled an address on a slip of paper and handed it to him. "Steak or lamb chops?"

He smiled at her. "Surprise me," he said.

"There's an important thing you can do," she said. "Most of what I know about Mac's professional life is privileged information. Can you or the Senator get to the special prosecutor?"

"Max Larkin? Surely the Senator can."

"Then have the Senator tell Mr. Larkin who you are and what you want, and have Mr. Larkin call me and give me the green light to talk to you; or at least tell me what's taboo. This is a town flooded by leaks. I want to be sure mine are authorized." She held out her hand, and her handshake was firm, almost masculine. Cotter knew it was an affectation of women who work in what used to be called a man's world. "Seven o'clock?" she asked.

"I look forward, Miss Branson," he said.

"For God sake, David, didn't I say no formality? It's Maggie."

* * *

Max Larkin, the special prosecutor, was a wiry, dark little man, egg-bald, very intense. He seemed to be a man in a perpetual hurry and as a matter of fact he was; in a hurry to reveal a malignant corruption at the heart of things. The Senator had talked to him, and Larkin had suggested that Cotter drop by his office.

"Don't think I asked you to stop by because I don't trust the Senator," Larkin said, "because I don't." He grinned. "In this job you get to where you don't trust anyone. It's paranoid. The hell of it is that most of the time you shouldn't trust anyone. Farraday comes pretty close to being an exception. Just what do you want, Cotter?"

"The Senator must have told you we don't buy the 'crazy little girl' theory, even though we know she pulled the trigger. So who sold her on the idea she was being a heroine? Most logical place to start looking seems to be here with his job on your staff. Who was he about to nail? Who had he nailed who might want revenge? What did he have on someone that hadn't yet surfaced?"

"There are something like seventeen thousand pages of transcribed testimony," Larkin said. "It would take you forever."

"I know. Talking freely with Margaret Branson could cut through miles of documents. She'd know who Crenshaw might have been worried about, the highlights of his work for you. I hope you'll tell her she can talk to me, or, if there are things that mustn't be mentioned, what they are."

Larkin smiled, a bitter little smile. "I want the same answers you do," he said. "If Mac's assassination *is* connected with this office, then you know something? I could be next."

"I'd thought of that," Cotter said.

Larkin shifted in his chair. "You know Mac had taken a leave of absence from my staff? He'd put everything pretty well in order, closed out the book, passed along the details of anything that was going on to Ed McMaster who's taking over for him. I'll tell Maggie she's free to tell you anything she chooses —on one condition."

"Which is?"

"The first hint you get that ties Mac's death to this office, the smallest breath of suspicion, you pass it on to me. I don't enjoy looking back over my shoulder every time I appear in public."

"It's a promise," Cotter said.

At exactly seven o'clock that evening Cotter turned up at Maggie Branson's apartment building and rang the buzzer in the front vestibule.

There was no answer.

Cotter glanced at his watch. Right on time. He tried the buzzer again, holding his finger on it steadily. Something must have held her up. He leaned against the wall, looking out through the glass top of the front door. He had brought a bottle of vintage Burgundy with him, and it was tucked under his arm. It should go with either steak or lamb chops.

There was no question about this being the right address. Her name was on the buzzer board—M. BRANSON.

Then he saw her. She was running toward the building, carrying what he assumed was a bag of groceries. She was running, not up the sidewalk, but from the far corner diagonally across the street itself. A taxi horn blared angrily as the driver had to swerve around her to keep from hitting her.

She stumbled as she started up the steps to the vestibule and Cotter was there to steady her.

She looked up at him, eyes wide. "Thank God you're here," she said. "I thought you might have taken off by now."

It wasn't, he was certain, the fear of missing a date that had turned her face so white.

"Take it easy," he said.

He took the bag of groceries from her while she fumbled, almost awkwardly, in her purse for a key. She got the door open and without a word led the way up the stairs to the second floor front apartment, opened that door, switched on lights, and went in. He followed her in and put the grocery bag and the wine down on a center table. She was leaning against the wall, trying to catch her breath.

"What is it?" he asked.

"I—I panicked," she said. "I—I've been followed before, but I always thought it was because I had good legs. But tonight—well, maybe it was because of Mac, and you, and what Mr. Larkin said to me on the phone—"

"What did Larkin say to you?"

"That if Mac was killed because of something he was doing on the special prosecutor's staff, I could be on the list of 'next victims' along with him. It was late when I left my office. I had to get to the market to buy our dinner, and I was hurrying. Then I saw him, like some character in an old Warner Brothers movie. Dark suit, dark hat, brim pulled down. If I'd been walking casually, I probably wouldn't have noticed him, but I was almost running and I saw he was keeping pace about twenty yards behind me. I—I guess I was spooked."

"It's a nasty sensation to be followed by someone you don't know," Cotter said. He moved toward the front windows of the apartment.

"Anyway, I stopped abruptly to look in a store window. He stopped, too. Then I knew for certain. The market was just a block further on." Maggie was beginning to breathe more evenly. "I went in, bought what I needed. He hadn't followed me into the market, which was thinning out of customers. It was almost closing time. That's why I'd been hurrying in the first place. The manager knows me, and I told him some goon had been annoying me out on the street. Could I slip out the back way? He offered to walk me home, but I wasn't that scared—I thought.

"I went out the back way, walked a block, and there he was! Then I'd really had it and I ran. Nearly got knocked down by a taxi as you probably saw."

"About five foot eight, a hundred and eighty pounds?" Cotter asked at the window.

"Sounds about right. Is he there?"

"Across the street," Cotter said. He crossed to Maggie, put his hands on her shoulders, and smiled down at her. "Get the broiler going for that dinner. It won't take me long."

"David!"

"I'll be very polite with him," Cotter said.

He went out and down the stairs to the vestibule. The man stood under an awning that protected the front window of a small bookstore. Cotter went out, down the front steps, and headed directly across the street. The man must have seen him coming but he couldn't know, Cotter thought, that he was Cotter's target. Just as Cotter was reaching the curb the man, hands in his coat pockets, turned to look in at the bookstore's dimly lit display. Two long strides and Cotter's arm was around the man's throat. He knew just how to apply the pressure.

"I was taught in the army how to kill when I got in a fight," he said quietly. "Take your hands out of your pockets, very slowly, so I can see them." He had felt the man's instant tension. Now he felt him relax as he slowly took his gloved hands out of his pocket and held them out from his stocky body.

"Turn around," Cotter said, loosening his arm from the man's throat.

The man turned, a dark, anonymous-looking fellow.

"Why are you following Miss Branson?" Cotter asked.

"Can I put my hands down?"

"At your sides, but not in your pockets. And don't try anything fancy. I'm so good at karate it should frighten you."

"Oh, I know all about your special skills, Mr. Cotter," the man said. He smiled at the surprise he saw on Cotter's face. "If you'll let me reach into my inside pocket, I'll show you some identification."

"What kind of identification?"

"FBI," the man said.

"Reach," Cotter said, "but very carefully. I get nervous in this kind of situation."

The man reached and brought out a wallet. In it was a card which identified him as Arthur Austin, an agent of the Federal Bureau of Investigation. Cotter looked at it, handed it back.

"I'll try again," he said. "Why are you following Miss Branson?"

"Orders," Austin said.

"How do you know about me, my name?"

"I was briefed. They have a whole book on you, Cotter."

"Maybe I should be flattered," Cotter said.

"We're always interested in people who try to do our job for us," Austin said. "Tell Miss Branson I'm sorry if I frightened her. I was just doing my job."

"I'm going to check out on you and your assignment," Cotter said.

"I would expect you to," Austin said. "The lady bought a very expensive steak. Have a good dinner."

There was nothing else to say or do. Cotter turned and walked back across the street to the apartment. Maggie answered his buzz instantly. She was waiting for him at the open apartment door.

"I saw it all from the window," she said. "He seemed to satisfy you, David."

"FBI," Cotter said.

"Why?"

"He told me you bought a very good steak," Cotter said.

43

"Put it under the broiler and I'll find out while it's cooking."

He dialed a number he knew by heart. It was Senator Farraday's private, unlisted number. The Senator must have been sitting by the phone because he answered at once. Cotter told him about Austin and asked to have the matter checked with the Director of the FBI.

"I want to know why Margaret Branson is being followed," Cotter said.

"And you," Farraday said.

"He wasn't following me, but someone may be. This Austin knew me by sight. Will you call me back at Maggie's apartment if you get anything?"

"As soon as I can locate the Director," Farraday said.

Maggie was in the kitchen, an apron tied around her simple little three-hundred-dollar black dress. The steak was sizzling under the broiler. She was working on a salad in a wooden bowl.

"Six minutes," she said. "Can you make a six-minute martini, David? Or would you prefer something else?"

"Martini would be fine."

"Makings in that corner cabinet," Maggie said. "Ice cubes in the box."

"Dry?" he asked. "For myself I make what I call an in-and-out. Pour vermouth in the shaker, swirl it around, pour it out and add gin."

"Wow!" Maggie said. "I'll try anything once."

When the drinks were ready, she turned the steak. She perched herself on the edge of the kitchen table. She tasted. "Heaven!" she said.

He smiled at her. "You were right about your legs," he said. "But calling them 'good' is an understatement." He looked at her over the rim of his glass. "Were you in love with Mac Crenshaw?" he asked.

"That's a low blow, David," she said, and turned toward the stove.

44

"All I want is a yes or no," he said. "When we start talking about him, I need to know your perspective. I need to know how you're looking at him."

She peeked into the oven at the steak. Then she turned and faced him. She lifted her glass and drank, almost to the bottom. "Would you believe me," she asked, "if I told you I don't know? But if you're asking me if I was Mac's mistress, the answer is no. Now hand me that platter on the table."

The steak was ambrosia, the salad a work of art, the wine he'd brought just right. She talked quite casually about Mac Crenshaw as if he hadn't asked the question. She had been part of a stenographic pool in the offices of one of the Crenshaw corporations. When Mac came back from Vietnam, she was assigned to him.

"It was like going to work for a movie star," she told Cotter. "He'd been all over the newspapers—the black-market trial, the social columns that covered his glamorous party goings and party givings, the pictures of his lovely dark wife and the fabulous house in Virginia. And he was fun to work for, David. He liked to laugh. He was deeply involved in his job and very good at it, but he wasn't intense and shut off like a lot of young career men in this town. I guess he had so much going for him that he wasn't afraid of anyone. There are damn few men in Washington, David, who aren't afraid of someone. I guess I hero-worshiped him. I may have had some fantasies about him in the early days. I felt I became more than just an employee. I was a friend. I was invited to parties. I helped Gwen, his wife, with invitation lists." A faintly bitter smile moved her lips. "I was taken for granted, but in a nice way. When he took the job with the special prosecutor, I moved over there with him. But I wasn't any longer the secretary who typed his letters. I was an executive assistant. I consulted with him about his job, like a staff officer to a general. I was proud of him and of the job. I don't mind telling you that I looked forward to the day

45

when I might be executive secretary to the President of the United States."

"So there must have been some other man in your life," Cotter said. "There's nothing of the old maid about you, Maggie."

She smiled at him oversweetly. "That, my dear David, is none of your goddam business."

The telephone rang.

"That may be the Senator getting back to you," she said.

Cotter took the call on the phone in the little dining alcove. It was Farraday. As he listened, all the good humor faded from Cotter's face, and it was set in hard lines.

"Thanks, Senator," he said finally, and put down the phone. He looked across the table at the expectant Maggie. "No one in the FBI has been assigned to cover you or me or anyone else connected with Crenshaw."

"But the man identified himself!"

"There was," Cotter said very quietly, "an agent named Arthur Austin. His body was fished out of the Potomac River about two weeks ago. Throat cut. Among the things not found on him were his gun, his identification. That bastard across the street had the identification, which involves him in the murder of the real Arthur Austin."

Cotter got up from the table and walked over to the front windows.

"He's gone, of course," he said. "But the chances are someone's taken his place. I'm going to get a man over here to stand guard over you, Maggie."

"David! You think—?"

"We're going to have to put off our talk," he said. "And I want to be sure you're safe, Maggie. You're too important to me."

3

A few years on the Senator's staff and another ten in his own business had supplied Cotter with a great many contacts of his own in Washington. The whole political society in the nation's capital is based on favors done and favors returned. Members of Congress are wooed by the lobbyists for big corporations and, in return for the right vote at the right time, receive financial backing when they come up for reelection. Leaks of information are paid for in kind. Insignificant to a voter in Squeedunk, Maine, is who sits next to his Senator at an embassy dinner. But it may be very important to some foreign diplomat who wants to bend the Senator's ear on such vital matters as the supply of arms or the price of oil. It is arranged through a hostess or a social secretary who will someday ask for a return favor from some other hostess or social secretary. It spirals up and down the ladder, from the bellhop who is assigned to the high-tipping corporation president to the call girl who gets the nod to accommodate a glamorous visiting movie star with certain perverse notions of sexual play. A favor in return for a favor in return for a favor.

"You owe me," Senator Farraday had said to Cotter. And it never occurred to Cotter not to pay.

Now it seemed that in attempting that payment he had stepped into some kind of booby trap. He had been blown up by a land mine once before in his life and he didn't intend to have it happen again. So, a favor for a favor.

It took Red Christie, Cotter's man, about forty minutes to show up at Maggie's apartment. When he saw Maggie, Christie looked pleased with the assignment.

"I'll keep in touch," Cotter said. "In the meantime, don't let anyone in here, not even your mother, Maggie." He turned to Christie. "This could be big-league violence, Red."

"I'm not sleepy," Christie said.

Maggie went to the door with Cotter. Her cool fingers touched his hands. "Is it as bad as you make it sound, David?"

He looked down into her anxious, gray-green eyes. He was surprised to find he thought of her as an old and cherished friend. "I'd rather overestimate than be careless," he said.

And what was the danger? That someone thought Maggie knew something that would lead to the man behind the gun. They, whoever "they" were, couldn't be certain that Maggie hadn't already passed that something along to Cotter.

The street outside Maggie's apartment seemed relatively quiet. There was no one outside the bookstore across the way. Cotter watched for a moment or two as a taxi and a few private cars crisscrossed in front of him. He stepped out onto the street and walked to the corner, every nerve tensed as he looked for someone who might or might not be there. At the corner he hailed a taxi and gave the address of the Weyland, the hotel where he was staying. He had made a call from Maggie's, and the man he'd called was waiting for him in the lobby. They went upstairs to Cotter's modest two-room suite.

Ted Garth looked like a prosperous young business executive, slim, dark, his gray flannel suit cut just a little on the mod side. He was actually an FBI agent. Not too long ago Cotter had slipped a piece of information to Garth which had helped wrap up a case for the FBI man. Now it was to be a favor for a favor.

Garth listened to Cotter's story, his face growing hard and dark when it came to the part about the impersonator of the dead agent, Arthur Austin.

"Sonofabitch," Garth said, when Cotter had finished.

"Tell me about Austin, what he was up to," Cotter said.

Garth lit a cigarette with hands that shook a little from anger. "A good man who hated the assignment he was on," he said.

"Sounds interesting."

"But off the record," Garth said.

Cotter smiled. "Where have I heard that before in this town?"

"Back in the Johnson and later the Nixon days," Garth said, "the Director was obsessed with the notion that all dissenters to the war in Vietnam were potential traitors and/or Communist agents. He was particularly hipped on the younger groups, the college campus demonstrators, the young people from the drug culture in the cities. Senator Farraday could give you chapter and verse on that. A lot of the old stuff has come before his committee in the last year or so."

"Get to Austin," Cotter said. "Someone may be planning to blow up this hotel while we talk."

Garth nodded and took a deep drag on his cigarette. "One of the ways of combating these youth groups was to infiltrate them. That was Austin's job, and he hated it. He was a baby-faced blond, ideally suited. He would move in on a group, he would screw the girls which was the custom of the country, he would make revolutionary speeches. Then, the part he hated most, he would set up some kind of action for them, lead them into it and right into the arms of the Bureau. He did that dozens of times in the last few years."

"That's still FBI policy? I thought, since Watergate—"

"When you work in the Bureau the right hand doesn't know what the left hand is doing," Garth said. "I assume it, because Art Austin was a friend, he hadn't changed his life style, his hippie look, and he was still bitterly complaining. When his body was fished out of the Potomac a couple of weeks ago, his throat cut, I took it for granted and so did the Bureau that he'd been caught out by whatever group he was at that moment infiltrating. That was the danger of his job, the risk he always knew he was running."

"And what group was he involved with when he died?"

"No idea," Garth said.

"Can you find out?"

"I can make a try," Garth said. "Someone in the Bureau must be trying to lower the boom on them."

Cotter got up from his chair and moved across the room, frowning. He stopped by the windows and looked down at the street. This was a busy part of town, much street traffic, many pedestrians coming and going. No one looked out of place. No one looked anchored anywhere. Cotter turned back.

"The girl who shot Mac Crenshaw was screaming something about stop poisoning the country when Bill Crenshaw clobbered her," he said. "Eighteen years old, the coroner said. It sounds like some sort of drug-culture kid."

"Art Austin had been dead two weeks when that happened," Garth said.

"I'd still like to know what group he was connected with then. I don't think the assassination was a spur-of-the-moment thing. It was probably planned for that place and that time well ahead. By luck we might identify the girl if we knew where to look."

"It would be a wild coincidence if the two things were connected," Garth said.

"The world is made up of wild coincidences," Cotter said. "Senator Farraday and I both believe someone programed that girl. We're trying to find out who. Along comes a stocky man with Arthur Austin's credentials interested in what Miss Branson is up to, what I'm up to. Would you think, in the face of that, that I'm reaching, Ted?"

"Maybe not," Garth said. "I'll help you reach."

*　　*　　*

It was about eleven o'clock when Garth left Cotter's hotel rooms. Eleven o'clock and noplace to go, Cotter thought. Garth would start an inquiry at the Bureau, but they'd be lucky to get anything before the next day. Cotter's next planned step, after Maggie Branson, had been to talk to the Crenshaw family. Mac Crenshaw's wife, the lovely dark-haired Gwen, was probably at Mac's Virginia home, for tomorrow was to be her husband's funeral. The President had decided that Mac Crenshaw should be buried at Arlington, along with the other martyrs in the fight for freedom. Mac's father and his brother Bill were probably in Washington, ready for the next day's ceremony. It wasn't a time to talk to any of them, but to sit still, doing nothing, was intolerable.

He called Maggie. "How sleepy are you?" he asked.

"Are you kidding?" There was an edge of hysteria to her voice.

"I've got things moving," he said. "If you're not ready to hit the sack, we could still talk a little."

"Please come back, David," she said.

Cotter took a taxi directly to the door of Maggie's apartment building. There were no suspicious-looking strollers, no one parked under the bookstore awning. He paid the driver and went into the vestibule. He rang the buzzer under Maggie's name and there was an instant clicking of the front door lock.

Maggie was waiting for him at the apartment door. She'd changed into some sort of loose-fitting pale yellow housecoat, and she looked suddenly very young because of a pair of horn-rimmed glasses and a little smudge of dirt at the side of her nose. Over her shoulder he saw the living-room table stacked with folders, papers, notebooks. She looked like a college girl caught doing her homework.

"Anything?" she asked.

"A vague lead," he said. He took his handkerchief out of his pocket and handed it to her. "You've got dirt on the side of

51

your nose, Miss Branson."

She laughed, pushed the glasses up onto her forehead, used his handkerchief effectively. "I've been going through a lot of stuff that doesn't seem very useful," she said, gesturing toward the table.

Red Christie was sitting in a comfortable armchair by the bookcases that lined the far wall. He had a book opened in his lap.

"Improve each shining hour," he said. He put the book back on the shelf and stood up. Christie was a young, former Washington city cop who'd been dropped from the force for the overenthusiastic handling of a prisoner. He'd been working for Cotter for three years now, and Cotter trusted and liked him.

"I just made a fresh pot of coffee," Maggie said.

"I'd love some," Cotter said.

As she brought him a cup, hot and black, he told her and Christie about his conversation with Garth. "It's far out," he said, "but Austin was working with the kind of groups to which the girl who killed Mac Crenshaw might have belonged. My man outside the bookstore, with Austin's credentials, must have had some connection with Austin's murder. How else could he have Austin's identification? And why was he interested in Maggie and me? It could only be because we're looking for answers he didn't want us to find. The only thing we're looking for is the identity of the girl. The tie-in simply can't be a coincidence."

Christie's Scotch-Irish face was twisted into a concentrated frown. "It could be something else," he said. "Your man outside the bookstore wasn't a youth movement type, was he?"

"Far from it."

"It could be he was concerned with other things that Maggie knows about Crenshaw's work for Max Larkin, the special prosecutor. It could have no connection with the assassination."

52

"What Farraday calls my 'built-in radar system' tells me it does," Cotter said.

"So we have to prove it or disprove it," Christie said. "You plan to stay here for a while?"

"If Maggie isn't too tired to talk," Cotter said.

"Do you imagine I could sleep?" she asked.

"I'd like to take a look around the neighborhood," Christie said. "Your bookstore man is probably miles from here, but he can have been replaced. Maybe I can find someone hanging around, or parked in a local bar."

"But you don't know who to look for," Maggie said.

Christie grinned at her. "Experience tells me that people who don't want to be noticed are usually very noticeable. Okay with you, David?"

"Good idea, I think," Cotter said. "Don't let him know if you spot him. We'll need him to lead us somewhere."

Christie left, and Cotter stretched out in a deep upholstered armchair. His body ached with fatigue. He'd been on a steady go for more than forty-eight hours.

"In addition to you, Maggie," he said, "I plan to talk to Mac Crenshaw's family; his wife, his father, his brother. But I thought that would have to wait till after the funeral tomorrow."

"Eleven o'clock at the Cathedral," she said.

"Since you haven't come across anything hot in those papers and documents, tell me about the family."

She took off her glasses and put them down on top of a pile of papers. "The trouble with all this stuff is, David, I don't know what I'm looking for." She moved, restlessly, around the room, the yellow chiffon clinging to her. "I'd better begin with the one I know least about, Ross Crenshaw, Mac's father. Oh, I know his reputation. Would you believe that in ten years of working for Mac I only met the old man twice that I can remember. Once at Mac's wedding reception, once when he came to see Mac at the office about something."

"You were working for Mac before he was married?" Cotter asked.

"About two years," she said. "I thought of the old man as a sort of a cliché. An old-fashioned industrial pirate, almost belonging to another century."

"A lot of today's conservatives seem to be taking dead aim at President McKinley," Cotter said.

Maggie smiled. "Your man Farraday isn't exactly a revolutionary," she said. "Ross Crenshaw wouldn't be backing him if he were."

"I may not agree with the Senator's politics," Cotter said, "but I believe in his honesty."

"Ross Crenshaw only believes in power," Maggie said. "His politics simply involve getting the right men in high places who will serve him the way he wants to be served."

"Mac would have been his ultimate success," Cotter suggested.

"This is the kind of power most Americans don't really believe exists," Maggie said. "CrenAm, the corporate name for Crenshaw-American, started with oil and over the years has sucked in copper, steel, chemicals, plastics, airlines, merchant fleets, newspaper chains, television stations. Name it and CrenAm owns it, controls it, or has the assets to bargain for it. Exclude the United States, Russia, and China, and CrenAm is more powerful than any other three nations put together."

"A slight exaggeration?" Cotter asked, smiling.

"If anything, an understatement," Maggie said. "Would you like some brandy in that coffee?" She'd stopped by the little chromium-trimmed bar in the corner of the room.

"Lovely idea," Cotter said.

She talked as she poured a measured serving into his cup. "Ross Crenshaw is raw power, so great that it's almost hard to think of him as a man with human feelings. Yet he is sitting

54

down in the Virginia house tonight surrounded by the ashes of a forty-year dream. I think he planned that Mac would be President the day he was born. If he had the capacity to love, it was centered on Mac." Maggie looked at Cotter, her eyes clouded. "We're not the only ones looking for the 'man behind the gun,' David. Ross Crenshaw's army of industrial spies, strong-arm goons, rulers of countries and captains of industry who depend on him, are looking for that man. When the old man finds him, he will destroy him brutally and everyone connected with him to the ends of the earth. Your friend, the Senator, wants to find him because it would satisfy his sense of justice and help him politically. Ross Crenshaw wants revenge. He wants to see the killer's blood, hear his screams of agony." Maggie was gripping the edge of the bar and her whole body was trembling. "That's Ross Crenshaw. If he is grieving for Mac tonight, it is only a secondary emotion. He is burning for revenge. No one thwarts a goal of his without paying double." She raised a pony of brandy and drank it, not adding it to her coffee. "He's a terrifying creature, David."

He was astonished at the intensity of her feeling. "There was a wife, the mother of the two boys."

"And a daughter who died in a riding accident when she was twelve," Maggie said. "Crenshaw's children had to take the highest jumps, the biggest risks. They had to be supermen and superwomen. Irene Crenshaw broke her neck attempting a jump an Olympic champion would have hesitated trying. Ross Crenshaw was standing at the paddock rail, urging the girl on, when she was killed." Maggie's lips trembled. "He was standing by urging Mac on when that crazed girl blew his brains out."

"The wife—Mac's mother," Cotter said.

Maggie reached for a cigarette and lit it. "She died when Irene, the youngest child, was quite young. Mac never spoke about her. There are rumors—"

55

"What sort of rumors?"

"That she died in some sort of mental institution. I—I had a feeling that no one could have stayed married to Ross Crenshaw and kept her sanity."

"From what I know of him Mac Crenshaw doesn't seem to have been like his father."

The change of subject seemed to relax Maggie. She came across the room and sat down on the arm of the couch, facing him. "Not alike at all. All Ross Crenshaw wants is power. Mac liked to be admired for his skills. He was great at sports, you know. Was proud of his educational accomplishments. He was a Rhodes scholar. He was proud of his skills in the law. He didn't have to clobber people to be liked, be loved. He was fun. He liked to laugh. He was witty. He was quite a guy, David."

"And you loved him?"

"Not in a romantic way. But I loved him as a friend."

"How would he have used the Crenshaw power if he'd come into it?"

"Oh, very differently, I imagine," Maggie said. She slid down onto the couch. "It's the history of big power, big fortunes, isn't it? The original Rockefeller was very different from his sons and grandsons. So much good done with money that came out of people in such a hard way in the beginning. The Ford fortune, doing so much good. I think Mac would have turned CrenAm in that direction if he—if he'd lived."

"And now the heir is William?"

"Bill is a whole other kettle of fish," Maggie said. "Mac was the glamor boy, Bill lived in his shadow. Mac was in the spotlight, nobody knew Bill was alive. There were the things that sometimes happen in that kind of relationship. He was kicked out of prep school for stealing! For God sake, the old man could have bought him Fort Knox if he'd wanted it. A psychiatrist would call Bill's stealing an attention-getter, I suppose. He quit college. A good student who wouldn't study. He went around the country, playing drums in a rock band. He wouldn't take any money from the old man. He was going to make it on his own."

"Not admirable?" Cotter asked.

Maggie shrugged. "Mac used to talk about it. A story about Bill would come from somewhere and the old man would blow his ever-loving stack! Bill arrested in some kind of tavern brawl somewhere; Bill in a police wagon along with some half-naked strippers; Bill in some kind of reckless speed chase that wound up in a wrecked car and the death of a girl passenger. Long list of things. Mac used to laugh and say that someday the Old Man would find a private Elba for Bill. Of course if Bill hadn't been a Crenshaw, he wouldn't have attracted so many cameras. And then, well, Bill changed."

"How?"

"About eight months ago he came home to live. The prodigal son, the fatted calf, the works. Wild oats sown, I suppose. Mac was surprised by him." Maggie frowned. "He couldn't guess what had changed Bill so abruptly. Bill, who had always sneered at Mac, jeered at him—out of jealousy and frustration, I suppose—was suddenly the loving, almost hero-worshiping brother. Mac wondered about it, but of course he was pleased. When Mac took a leave of absence from the special prosecutor and planned to go on the stump for your Senator, Bill became part of his staff, eager, helpful, efficient from all accounts. In the end he was within a split second of saving Mac's life, and did revenge his killing."

Cotter picked up his coffee cup, saw that it was empty, and put it down again. Maggie moved quickly to it, the yellow chiffon swirling around her. She moved very gracefully, Cotter thought.

"Would you prefer a highball, David?" she asked.

"Coffee and brandy is fine."

He watched her go into the kitchenette. He was very tired,

very relaxed, and yet he felt an unfamiliar stirring in him that he chose not to define. She brought him back his coffee, and the aroma of brandy was rich and reviving. What Maggie had told him about Ross Crenshaw and Bill made it obvious that they would be working toward the same objective as Farraday, but a bloodier and more violent end if they identified the man behind the gun. Ross Crenshaw, if he would talk, might be much closer to motives for the assassination than anyone else. Killing Mac might have been a way to hurt the father for some reason hidden away from the rest of them. Ross Crenshaw might be willing to point the way if he thought Cotter could help him.

"What about Mac's wife?" Cotter asked. The brandied coffee went down, warm and rewarding.

Maggie turned away toward the bar and poured herself a neat slug of Scotch. Then she turned back to him with a wry little smile. "Women aren't as good about women as they are about men," she said.

"Particularly women who are involved with the same man, even if in different ways," Cotter said.

"You keep insisting I must have been more to Mac than his executive assistant!" she said.

"It would help to be sure," he said. "I'd know—"

"Damn you, David," she said. "Do you want to know about Gwen or not?"

"Your version of her," he said, smiling.

She moved away from him, beginning to roam the room again. "Poor little rich girl," she said. "Beautiful. She will take your breath away when you see her. Always beautifully groomed, looking highly sophisticated. Yet in many ways she's just a little girl. She doesn't like big social gatherings. Mac loves to shine his light in them. He is always the star of the occasion. She shrinks from them. He loves sports, loves to play games, go to games." Cotter noticed that Maggie spoke of him as though he was alive, as if she'd forgotten what had happened in Brownsville. "She has no interest in sports."

"What brought them together? If their interests were so dissimilar, what?" Cotter asked.

She stood with her back to him. "That's a kindergarten question," she said.

"The Lassiters, Gwen's family, are very rich," Cotter said, "but Mac didn't need to marry for money."

"Because she was so beautiful," Maggie said, "he wanted to make love to her forever and ever."

"Was she any good at it?" Cotter asked quietly.

Maggie spun around. Her color was high. "How the hell am I supposed to know that?"

"Because you were closer to him than almost anyone else. Because you must have sensed his disappointments, his needs."

"Well, I don't know!"

"It has been suggested to me that there might have been many other women in his life, other men in hers," Cotter said.

"So there may have been other women. About Gwen and men I don't know. I never heard a hint of it."

"And you were one of Mac's other women," Cotter said.

"Damn you, David! Yes!" She almost shouted it. "Once. Just once! I went on a business trip to Dallas with him and— and it happened. But that was all, that one time."

"Why only once? Was Gwen what he really wanted?"

"It was only once because that's how it had to be for me. Oh, he wanted me. But I couldn't go on with it."

"Why?"

"Because I'd have become an addict! That's why!"

She turned away again and he guessed she was hiding tears. He wondered why he had pressed her so hard. A man's mistress can reveal things that no one else can. Was that why he'd kept after her, or had he needed to know for another reason?

"I know what it's like," he said after a long silence. "I was

59

married for just a year, and it was perfect, and then Marjorie died. You're full of hungers after that that nothing will satisfy. You're obsessed by dreams that you can't make come to life. I know how tough it is. You're dying of hunger, with all kinds of delicacies around you, and you can't—you can't satisfy your needs."

Her shoulders were shaking, but she didn't speak.

"You're afraid to try," he said, "for fear it will destroy the perfection you remember."

She turned very slowly and faced him. "I'd like to try, David," she said.

Which was how it happened.

Two pasts were for one night obliterated by a marvelous, mutual present. No comparisons were made. It was as though they had been created exactly for each other and no one else. It was as if each movement had been magically choreographed, as if each touch satisfied an undreamed-of need, as if all pain could be wiped out by an understanding of giving and taking, as if they had practiced forever to find perfection—a perfection that was there with the first joining of lips, the first meeting of body with body.

And then, for Cotter, there was something he hadn't known for years. There was sleep—deep, drugged, rewarding. It was sleep that began tangled with another person, a beloved, sharing person. And then blessed darkness.

He woke with the morning sun shining brightly in his eyes. She was gone, but he could hear her moving about in the next room. She appeared in the doorway. She was wearing a plain black dress, a small black hat, gloves. She came over and stood by the bed.

"I'm going to be late for the services at the Cathedral," she said.

He was startled. He glanced at his watch on the bedside

60

table. It was a quarter past ten. He had slept for nearly nine hours.

She spoke in a flat sort of voice. "If you don't want to see me again, David, I'll understand."

The whole wonder of what had happened swept over him. "Not want to see you?" His voice was husky.

"If it didn't do for you what you hoped it would—"

"Oh, my God, Maggie! If I could just find the words—"

She smiled. She sat down on the edge of the bed and reached for his face, cupped it in her gloved hands. "My dear David," she said. "Incredibly, miraculously, marvelously I love you. I love you, love you."

She bent down and kissed his lips, but when he reached for her, she pulled away. She laughed. "I'll be late for church," she said. "I'll see you when it's over."

"Where?"

"Here, or anywhere in God's world you want, David."

And she was gone.

He lay there, the sunlight warm on his bared chest. She would be back soon; she would be back soon. And then, as if someone had hit him in the face with a pitcher of ice water, he sat bolt upright in bed. He was on a job! He should be at the Cathedral, watching who came, seeing which public figures might show a too pious concern. He should have set up a surveillance of the ceremony. He had intended to—before Maggie.

And where the hell was Red Christie? Probably come back, gotten no answer to a ring at the doorbell, and diplomatically tiptoed away. Cotter knew he wouldn't have heard the doorbell after the magical interlude with Maggie. His sleep had been so deep he wouldn't have heard a summons from the angel Gabriel. Maggie, blessed Maggie, wouldn't have allowed the moment to be interrupted.

Later, racing through the streets in a taxi, he found himself wondering why Red Christie hadn't broken in the door. He was supposed to be guarding Maggie, and no answer to the doorbell should have spelled the need for action.

But before that he had gone to the bathroom and found an injector razor and a tin of medicated shaving cream waiting for him on the washbasin. Instantly he turned juvenile. What sonofabitch kept shaving things here? What man? Then he was laughing at himself in the mirror. Most women used this kind of equipment. Silly clod, he was in love!

He was only ten or twelve minutes behind Maggie in arriving at the Cathedral. The brief service was already drawing to a close. The choir was singing a hymn, the voices of the boy sopranos high and eerie. From the rear of the church he saw that the mourners were distinguished. There was the President and the First Lady; there were judges and Senators and Congressmen and diplomats. There were men of great importance in the world of business, accompanied by their wives and children. Gwen Crenshaw was flanked by Ross Crenshaw and Bill Crenshaw. He couldn't see the widow's face to verify her beauty.

But he saw the little black hat atop the coppery red hair. Maggie was sitting in the pew behind the family. Cotter's heart jammed against his ribs. He spoke her name, softly, to himself, over and over. "Maggie, Maggie, Maggie!"

Then a hand like an iron claw grabbed his arm and spun him around, and he found himself facing Ted Garth, his FBI friend. Garth's face was white, his eyes bloodshot.

"Where the hell have you been?" he asked in a tense whisper.

"What do you mean, where have I been?"

"We've been looking for you since around two o'clock this morning," Garth said. "No one knew where to reach you or where you could be."

"What was so important?" Cotter asked, and suddenly knew

before the answer came.

"Your man Christie was found beaten to death in an alley on the north side. His body was stripped of identification, gun, whatever he might have been carrying. But one of the cops who found him recognized him from his days on the force. You know what he was up to?"

Cotter drew a deep breath. "He was protecting me," he said bitterly.

Part Two

The Game Players

1

Down the marble steps from the entrance to the Cathedral a company of marines in dress uniform stood at attention, waiting to escort Mac Crenshaw's coffin to the cemetery. Cotter stared down at them, his vision a little blurred. You were safe as hell when you were dead! They sent out the marines to protect you when it no longer mattered. They sent out the cops, the Bureau men, to find the truth—after you were dead. The FBI and the Washington cops would be after whoever killed Red Christie, but it wasn't going to do Red any good. He was dead, God save us! And all the efforts of the FBI, and the State Police, and Ross Crenshaw's empire, and Senator Farraday and his private investigator, David Cotter, weren't going to do Mac Crenshaw one damn bit of good. The marines, the sun shining on their buckles, were about to take him to where men with shovels would, figuratively, throw dirt in his face. And day after tomorrow those same men would throw dirt in Red Christie's face under less elaborate circumstances. "All the king's horses and all the king's men/Couldn't put Humpty together again."

"But I am alive, and Maggie is alive, and I goddamned well intend to keep it that way!" Cotter said.

Garth had guided him out of the Cathedral, out onto the steps. He still had his tight grip on Cotter's arm.

"Make sense!" Garth said, his voice harsh.

"I found something I thought I'd never find again," Cotter said, "and in the process I let Red down. I should have been out looking for him when he didn't come back. I might have got to him before it was too late."

"You were with the Branson dame?" Garth asked, sounding surprised. "I called you there. I thought you might have gone back there. Why didn't you answer the phone?"

Cotter made an almost threatening gesture as he wrenched himself free of Garth's hold on his arm. "There was no phone, not in the world I was living in just then. I wasn't supposed to be listening for a phone."

Inside the choir voices rose, swelled.

Ted Garth wasn't an insensitive man. Cotter, he realized, had been in bed with a girl, but it hadn't been an inconsequential one-night stand. This wasn't the time for a wisecrack.

"You say he was protecting you, David?"

Cotter nodded. "In a sense. I had him there to guard Maggie Branson before I set out to talk to you. After I left you I went back there. Maggie had a lot of Mac Crenshaw's files and records in her apartment. I wanted to talk to her about them, about the Crenshaw family, about anything that would give me a starting point toward what I told you—'the man behind the gun.' The fellow with Austin's credentials was gone, of course, but Red and I thought he might have been replaced by someone who was keeping Maggie under surveillance. Red went out to scout around the neighborhood."

"And he didn't come back?"

Cotter turned his head from side to side as though he was in pain. "There's no way I can explain this to you, Ted, so that you'll understand. I lost my wife several years ago, the most precious person on earth to me. There's never been anyone since. There's been a hunger so deep I can't describe it to you. Maggie had something of the same sort of problem. It came out, both our stories, while we talked. Suddenly there was an answer to what we both needed, not planned for, not dreamed of." Cotter's mouth was dry. "Yesterday at this time I didn't know her. Today she's all that matters to me. All! And she's in danger, Ted. What happened to Christie tells us just how great that danger is!"

"Try to forget about romance for a minute," Garth said, "and remember that you're a good, skilled, professional investigator. She'd need your help if she was just Miss X. Professional help, not the help of a lover."

A cold disinterested voice interrupted them. "You'll have to move out of the way, gentlemen."

Behind the voice was the sound of the Cathedral organ in the deep notes of the funeral march. The procession, with the important pallbearers carrying Mac Crenshaw's coffin, was coming out into the open. The marines were at attention, rifles at the present arms.

Garth had to move Cotter out of the way.

The bearers and the coffin went past them. Senator Farrady was one of the bearers, stone-faced. And then came Gwen Crenshaw, dark, pale, as beautiful as Maggie had reported, her head held high and proud. Behind her was a gray-haired old man, bent, black glasses hiding his eyes. He leaned heavily on the arm of a good-looking young man. These had to be Ross Crenshaw and his son Bill. Then came other members of the family, unidentifiable to Cotter. And then there was Maggie, the copper-colored hair suddenly glittering in the sunlight.

Cotter stepped forward, put his arm around her, and, almost roughly, pulled her out of the procession.

"David!" she protested. "I have to go on with—"

"Red Christie was murdered while we were together," he said.

"Oh, my God, David!"

Her fingers were hooked into the lapels of his jacket.

"I want to get you out of here quickly," Cotter said.

"But, David, I have to—"

"You have to come with us now, at once," Cotter said. "This is Ted Garth, a friend. He is also an FBI agent."

Garth and Maggie muttered something to each other.

"David! About Christie—?" Maggie asked.

His arm still around her, Cotter swept her down the wide, stone Cathedral steps, but away from the funeral cortege. There may have been someone in the procession who took special note of Margaret Branson. Cotter knew that, and he wanted to get her away before anyone could regroup his forces.

A loitering taxi was the way of escape. They got in, Maggie sitting between the two men. Both Maggie's hands were clinging to Cotter's. He gave an address.

"My office!" Maggie said.

"Listen to me, love," he said. His voice was low and intense. "You were followed last night by a man who turned out to have a dead man's credentials. It was Ted, here, I went to see when I knew the man outside the bookstore was a fake. When I came back, Red Christie went out to scout the neighborhood. He was found beaten to death in an alley not far from your apartment about two this morning."

"But why, David?"

"Red was an ex-cop," Cotter said. "He saw someone he knew, or knew about. They couldn't let him report back to me or to anyone else. So they killed him. Now remember, this starts with a man following you, love." His hands tightened around Maggie's.

"I don't understand, David. I don't understand what I—"

"You were Mac Crenshaw's confidential secretary," Garth said in a flat voice.

70

Maggie looked at him, her gray-green eyes bewildered.

"You may know something that would lead to what David calls 'the man behind the gun.' "

"But I don't!"

"You don't know what you know," Cotter said. "Behind you are ten years of working for Mac. There are papers, records, files on old cases, conversations about people and places, deals, plea bargains, God knows what. Your mind isn't a computer, Maggie. You can't just press a button and come up with a name, a situation, a long-forgotten something. But as you go through the records, the files, as you're asked questions by some inquisitive jerk like me, something terribly dangerous to someone could pop into focus. Something that at this moment you don't know that you know. You're being watched at the moment to make sure you haven't remembered or found the dangerous thing. If Red Christie could have told us who he saw, that might have cued you in. Your life is that close to being on the line, Maggie."

"But I don't know anything, David!" It was a whisper.

"I think David has an idea what we'll find when we get to your office," Garth said.

"Find?"

"Your files, your records, your notebooks, your business diaries," Cotter said. "They will have been ripped apart, maybe even carted away so they could be gone through at their leisure."

"The same thing at your apartment," Garth said.

"But how could they risk—?"

"This is the one time they could be absolutely certain you wouldn't be in either place," Cotter said. "You would be at Mac's funeral; at the Cathedral and at the cemetery. At least a couple of hours of certain free time for them."

"If they find what's dangerous to them in your papers and

records, Miss Branson, then they'll know that sooner or later you'll remember," Garth said. "They'll have to make sure that doesn't happen."

"Oh, my God," she said. It wasn't believable.

"And if they don't find what they're looking for, they'll try to get you away somewhere and force you to remember," Cotter said. "And when you do remember—if you do remember—it won't be safe for them to let you go."

"But what do I do, David?"

"Exactly what I tell you, love." He gave her a tight little smile. "I'm going to put you in a deepfreeze somewhere you won't be found."

"And then we watch for people who are looking for you, Miss Branson," Garth said.

"And we clobber the sonsofbitches!" Cotter said.

Both Maggie's office and her apartment were a shambles, as Garth had predicted. In the office, filing cabinets, desk drawers, an office safe had been looted, documents scattered around. Maggie, in a kind of trance, kept shaking her head to questions. There was no way to tell what might be missing without hours, maybe even days and weeks, of going through the wreckage. Ten years of office records!

"How could an accumulation of ten years be kept here?" Garth asked.

"Oh, every year or so Mac went through the files, packed away what he called 'ancient history' in cartons, had them taken away."

"Taken where?" Cotter asked.

"Storage—somewhere."

"You don't know where, love?"

"No, David. I assumed—"

"No warehouse receipts? No storage records?" Garth asked.

"Because there were none I assumed he simply took them

home to the Virginia house. There are all sorts of stables, barns, outbuildings there," Maggie said.

"That could be their next stop," Garth said.

There had been nothing in the office of value to steal except the records and files. There was a tape recorder and all the used tapes had been taken. They were the only things Maggie could be sure were gone.

"But there was nothing of any value on the tapes," she said. "He would dictate ordinary office correspondence for our typist to transcribe. Political invitations, answers of acceptance or regrets."

They used to laugh about the office safe. Mac kept liquor in it for unexpected guests. The people who had ransacked the place had left the liquor untouched.

The apartment was less of a shock than the office, only because they were certain now what they'd find. The stack of papers Maggie had brought home from the office had been swept up and carried off. Not a scrap left behind. There was evidence that her writing desk, bureau drawers, closets had been searched. Someone had been nice enough to leave things in pretty good order.

Garth thought there wasn't much point in having the two places fingerprinted. They were dealing with professionals.

"What now?" Maggie asked.

"What's happened here and at the office is excuse enough to justify our going to see the Crenshaw family, even though it is the day of Mac's funeral," Cotter said. "If Mac's 'ancient history' is stored in Virginia, someone may be on the way there to hunt for something."

Cotter had reduced his personal living style to the simplicity of a hotel room since his wife's death, but in other areas not involving the place where he slept he permitted himself certain luxuries. He had a rather extensive wardrobe, part of which he

73

considered a professional necessity. There were times in his business when he wanted to be completely inconspicuous, and times when he wanted to be noticed. He dressed to fit the needs of the moment, simple or flamboyant. One of his problems was that he was a look-alike. Too many people had the same reaction to him. He looked like a younger Burt Lancaster. Much of the time he had to deliberately conceal that likeness so that he wouldn't be remembered.

Beyond clothes, another area of self-indulgence was cars. He had been fascinated by motors when he was General Farraday's jeep driver in the army. He liked to tinker. After the army and as soon as he could afford it, he began buying used foreign cars and rebuilding them himself. It was a hobby. He was a superb driver. One summer vacation, when he'd gone back to college and Farraday was on a trip to the Far East, he'd earned a nice little chunk of money as a stunt driver for a movie company. One of his greatest pleasures was to find himself behind the wheel of a car with a self-tuned motor, headed for anywhere. In a garage near his office he kept a Mercedes brougham and a two-seated Ferrari with a souped-up engine. In the Ferrari he could outrun almost any kind of chase.

From Maggie's phone Cotter called the garage and ordered the Mercedes brought around to the apartment building.

"Pack a bag with what you'll need for a week or ten days," Cotter said to Maggie.

"But, David, I can't go anywhere. Closing out Mac's office. I have to finish that."

"You're not going to stay in this apartment, with or without protection," Cotter said. "You, my sweet, are going to disappear after we've visited the Crenshaws."

"David, I can't walk out on—"

He took her by the shoulders and literally shook her. "God damn it, Maggie, Mac Crenshaw is dead! Austin is dead! Red

Christie is dead! Do I have to spell it out for you in block letters? Pack a bag!"

Without a word she turned and walked down the hallway to the bedroom. Garth, his eyes narrowed, was watching Cotter.

"You can't carry her around with you if you want to get the job done," he said.

"I can't get the job done unless I know she's safe," Cotter said. The corners of his mouth moved in a small, twisted smile. "So help me, Ted, I haven't felt like this since my first high school girl friend. I was going to be a hero then."

"You're going to be a dead hero if you don't get your priorities straightened out," Garth said.

Cotter ignored that comment. "What about Austin and his job? I—I've forgotten to ask you about him."

"No dice just yet," Garth said. "The agent handling Austin and his assignment is a man named Wesley Moss. Good man. He's out of touch with the Bureau at the moment. As soon as he checks in I'll get to him. What do you plan to do after you see the Crenshaws?"

Cotter shrugged. "Who knows what they'll tell me?"

"Check with me," Garth said. "Finding the man who killed Austin is my job. Any lead I get may help you."

"Thanks, Ted. I'm going to need help."

Garth went to the door, and then turned back. "Watch your step with Ross Crenshaw," he said. "He may not want to help you, David."

"Why in God's name not?" Cotter said. "We're both after the same thing—the man responsible for Mac's death."

"Crenshaw won't want anyone to get in the way of his method of punishment," Garth said. "It won't be a legal method, you understand."

Garth left.

He couldn't have reached the downstairs vestibule when the

75

front doorbell buzzer rang. Cotter spoke into the intercom. It was the boy from the garage with the Mercedes.

"Stay with it, Benny, until I come down," Cotter said, "and I'll drive you back to the garage."

"I've got the garage motorcycle hooked to it, Mr. Cotter. I don't need you to drive me back."

"All the same, stay with the car till I come down, Benny. I don't want anyone messing with it."

"Okay, Mr. Cotter."

Then Maggie appeared from the bedroom, carrying one fairly large bag and a second smaller one. She put them down, looked around for Garth, and then came to Cotter. It was as if they had always been together, as though they had always been everything to each other. He took her in his arms and he could feel her body trembling. She was frightened. He kissed her gently.

"Maggie, Maggie," he said.

"I can't make it make sense, David," she said.

"We have options," he said. "We take a plane from here to wherever you say. Tahiti? We lie there in the sun for the rest of our lives. Mac Crenshaw's death is political. To hell with politics. To hell with the whole dirty business. Since last night nothing matters to me but us, Maggie."

She looked up at him, eyes wide. "If you could go, I'd go with you in a minute, David. But you can't go, and you know it. Mac's tragedy may be politics, but Red Christie was your friend. Did he have a family?"

Cotter nodded. "A wife and two small kids."

"So you can't go until you've squared things for them. I don't know you well, David, and yet I know you better than anyone in the world. You couldn't go if I begged you to."

It was true and he knew it. His arms tightened around her.

"I keep thinking there must be someplace I could send you, someplace I could hide you," he said. "And yet I keep telling

76

myself that, away from me, you wouldn't be safe. I could never be sure you were safe, and I could never get the job done."

"I want to stay with you if that's what you want," she said.

"It's the only way I can make it," he said.

Later he thought he must have been out of his mind to ask her to run such a risk.

If you have taste but no money, your sense of the fitness of things will show; if you have taste and all the money in the world, the result can be miraculous.

Mac Crenshaw had bought a house after he and Gwen Lassiter were married, Maggie had told Cotter. Mac had needed to be near Washington, and he'd probably bought a pleasant little bridal cottage, Cotter had imagined. It wasn't a cottage. It was a graceful, large colonial house surrounded by rolling fields and woods, and a collection of outbuildings— stables, a caretaker's cottage, a guest house on a distant hillside. A rail fence surrounded the perimeter of the property, acres and acres of it, and the main house itself was hidden from rubbernecking sightseers by a perfectly trimmed hedge ten feet high. It was a lovely retreat for the prince and the princess. When you are a Crenshaw or a Lassiter, Cotter thought, you rub the magic lamp and there it is, whatever you dreamed of.

Inside the high hedge things were not what would have passed for normal. There were a dozen or more cars. There were men in business suits who were clearly not the servants of the country squire. They made no effort to conceal the fact that they were armed.

Two of them stopped the Mercedes as it nosed into the driveway. No visitors today, Cotter and Maggie were told. Maggie explained that she was Mac Crenshaw's secretary and that it was urgent that she and Cotter talk to the Crenshaws. The men, like robots, weren't buying. Maggie identified Cotter as an aide to Senator Farraday. For some reason that seemed to carry weight. One of the men waved toward the house and a third man came down off the pillared front terrace. He was dressed in a funeral black cutaway.

"This one knows me," Maggie whispered to Cotter. "He's Mac's estate manager." Then she managed a smile. "Hello, Mr. Bishop," she said as the man looked down into the car.

"Oh, Miss Branson." A raised eyebrow asked a question about Cotter.

"David Cotter, an aide of Senator Farraday's," Maggie said.

"The Senator's here," Bishop said, as though the news might make Cotter turn tail and run.

"Something has happened that's very important the Crenshaws should know," Maggie said. "I know it's a bad time to come, but it's urgent, Mr. Bishop."

Bishop gave the robot-men an all-clear sign and Cotter drove the Mercedes to a parking spot another man indicated. He wondered if he'd be searched for concealed weapons or a bomb! The men looked as if they thought it was quite possible he had either or both. But Bishop ushered them through the front door and into the house. The entrance hall was cool and sunlit. There were paintings. Cotter recognized a Wyeth and another, stark and ominous, that he was certain was a Benton.

Off to the right there was the sound of subdued voices. The barbaric custom of feasting after a funeral was in progress. An elaborate buffet was laid out for friends and relatives. The funeral baked meats!

Bishop moved quickly away and came back with the good-looking young man Cotter had seen supporting Ross Crenshaw at the Cathedral. He was tall, slender, dark, with wire-rimmed glasses that gave him a scholarly look.

"Hello, Maggie," he said.

"Bill, this is David Cotter," she said.

Bill Crenshaw offered a moderately firm hand.

"Something has happened we thought ought to be reported to you," Maggie said. "Mac's office and my apartment have been ripped apart by someone searching for Mac's records. David is an aide of Senator Farraday's. We don't know what they took, if anything. I told David I thought Mac had stored old records out here."

"If they didn't find what they wanted in the office or in Maggie's apartment, this could be their next stop," Cotter said.

Bill Crenshaw gave him a shy smile. "If you saw that army out in the yard, David, you'll know that no one is going to steal anything out here; not while Father's in residence."

Easy first name; easy cordiality.

"We hoped you, or Gwen, or Mr. Crenshaw might be able to guess what they were looking for," Maggie said.

"I wouldn't have the foggiest," Bill said. "I don't suppose Gwen would either. I don't think Father will talk to you just now. He's gone up to his room. I think you can understand that he's quite literally in shock." The eyes behind the wire-rimmed glasses were very bright. "I should have thought you knew more about Mac's affairs, professional and social, than anyone else, Maggie."

"I'm guessing that Mac Crenshaw's assassination wasn't political," Cotter said.

The smile faded from Bill's face, and the eyes turned cold and hard. He was, Cotter thought, remembering the girl in the fur coat, the hand coming out of the fur muff, the gun, his attempt, seconds too late, to avert tragedy.

"What else if not political?" Bill asked. "He was campaigning, wasn't he?"

"Not for himself," Cotter said.

Bill's laugh was short, mirthless. "Maybe you think not, David. Mac was campaigning for himself eight years from now!"

79

"But getting himself killed helped Senator Farraday. It didn't hurt him."

"That screwy girl might have killed anyone that looked political," Bill said. "She wouldn't have had to know who he was. 'Stop poisoning the world!' That's crazy stuff, Manson stuff. Warped politics."

"Then who is searching Mac's files and why, Bill?" Maggie asked.

"Not kids," Cotter said. He described the man outside the bookstore; he told Bill what had happened to Red Christie. "The only tie-in to kids may be Austin. But if there is a tie-in, I think that girl was used by someone to make it look the way you think it looks, Bill."

"Does the Senator know all this?" Bill asked.

"Not all. Not the latest. He was at the funeral, and now here."

"I think you'd better tell him," Bill said. Again the faint, shy smile. "I'm supposed to take over Mac's job of helping the Senator's campaign. Frankly, I don't know yet which end is up."

Bill walked away toward the voices in the dining room. Maggie stood close to Cotter, holding onto his arm. "It's hard to believe," she said. "Four days ago there was a party here, a dance. Mac was so gay, riding the crest of the wave. He and Gwen were dancing together and they—they looked as though they owned the world!"

Cotter looked down at her. "It's hard to believe, but one day ago I didn't know you."

"David!"

Bill Crenshaw came back from the dining room and with him were Gwen Crenshaw and Senator Farraday.

"Maggie," Gwen said. They were friends.

The Senator introduced Cotter to the widow. The Senator's deeply lined face, so familiar to television viewers from the

80

hearings, was both angry and anxious.

"Bill's told me about your man Christie," he said. "This is getting out of hand, David."

"We can talk in Mac's study," Gwen said, gesturing across the entrance hall. "I'd like to be in on your briefing, Mr. Cotter. All of us here are determined to see justice done for Mac. It's all that matters to us just now."

She had a low, husky voice. Maggie, Cotter thought, was an enormously attractive woman; the coppery hair, the bright eyes, the aliveness. Maggie was Maggie, special. But Gwen Crenshaw was breathtaking in another way. The bones of her face had been sculptured by an artist; her dark hair, her deep violet eyes, her pale, flawless skin, her slim yet perfect figure, made it difficult to take your eyes away from her. Cotter understood now what Maggie had meant when she'd said it was a kindergarten question to ask what Mac had seen in this woman who shared none of his social enthusiasms. Yesterday, before Maggie, Cotter thought he would have had dreams about her. She moved with the grace of a dancer, and everything about her suggested a personal pride. There was courage here, too. She had not been floored by her husband's murder. She had come out of her corner fighting.

Mac Crenshaw's study was a very personal room. It didn't look like a work place. There were silver trophies Mac had won at golf and skiing; there were photographs of college teams he'd played on, of a golf match at St. Andrews in Scotland, of the ski run at St. Moritz with Mac taking a dizzying turn somewhere along the way; of Mac, wearing a broad grin, standing on the steps of the Supreme Court Building where he had just won a decision for the special prosecutor, Larkin in the background looking pleased. In one square of wall space was a picture of his wedding, with Gwen looking marvelous in a white lace wedding gown; a studio photograph of Gwen that didn't do her justice; a candid shot of Gwen in a scanty bathing suit, palm trees in the background.

There were no file cabinets, no desk that looked devoted to work of a serious sort. There was a hi-fi set in a far corner of the room with stacks of records in wire racks. There were books, mostly modern, in a case on one wall. This was not a place, Cotter thought, to look for evidence that was worth killing a man for.

At Farraday's suggestion Cotter brought them up to date on facts and on his theories. He found it hard to keep his eyes off Gwen. She sat in a straight-backed Windsor armchair, her long legs crossed. She listened with a kind of intense concentration to every word Cotter spoke.

"It's my opinion at the moment," Cotter said, concluding his statement, "that we're not dealing with politics in the obvious sense."

"Obvious?" Gwen's question was crisp, without emotion.

"A crazy girl, killing for some far-out reason involving pollution of some sort. 'Stop poisoning the world!' That may have been her motive, but it was used by someone else to get her to act. Mac Crenshaw wasn't running for office, so it wasn't to stop him for that reason. He wasn't a lawmaker who stood in the way of something the girl wanted. If anything, he was opposing political corruption, not fostering it."

"Maybe she was just out to kill anyone," Bill Crenshaw said. He was standing by the windows, looking down over the rolling countryside. "Kill for killing. An attention-getter. Mac was unlucky."

"Not in my book," Cotter said. "He was the intended target, no one else. Why search his office? Why search Maggie's apartment? Why have Maggie followed? Why kill my man Christie, who must have stumbled onto something? And why kill Austin, the FBI agent, who was involved with the kind of youth groups to which that girl might have belonged? Your

82

brother wasn't unlucky, Bill. He was meant to die. They were after him."

"But *why?*" Gwen leaned forward in her chair, her bright lips parted.

"When we know that, Mrs. Crenshaw, we'll know who," Cotter said. "Maggie and I came out here partly because we thought Mac may have stored old records out here from his office."

"He did," Bill said. "They're in cartons in the carriage house."

"Somebody may try to get at them," Cotter said.

"We can see to it that they don't," Bill said. "I hadn't thought they were important; closed files on closed cases. Probably the special prosecutor has duplicates, wouldn't you say, Maggie?"

"Case records are all with Mr. Larkin," Maggie said. "Mac's accumulation in his office was mostly personal correspondence, personal accounts. Nothing that I could see that would be of any real value to anyone. Of course when he was working on a case, he'd have everything relating to it that he needed. But Mac resigned from Mr. Larkin's staff almost a month ago to work for the Senator. Everything that was connected to the special prosecutor's work was long gone."

Cotter looked at Senator Farraday. "Was there anything connected with the campaign, Senator? Did you have something hot on somebody, some other candidate?"

"We're not running that kind of campaign," Farraday said.

"I'm not saying you'd use that kind of material, but you might have it. You have friends who might pass along gossip, even facts about someone."

"Nothing that I know of," Farraday said. "And I don't think Mac would have kept anything like that from me. We'd have discussed what to do about information of that sort."

"Bill?" Cotter asked.

"God, I haven't had a chance to go through Mac's things," Bill said. "He certainly never told me about anything."

"Mrs. Crenshaw?" Cotter focused on the widow's pale, still face.

For a moment he thought she hadn't been listening. Then the wide violet eyes turned his way. "Mac used to say that a good lawyer like a good athlete never brings the ball game home with him," she said. "He talked a little to me about the campaign. He was enthusiastic about it. He believed the Senator had a great chance to get the nomination and win the election in the fall. But the kind of things he told me were— well, funny things people said, jokes he'd heard, casual Washington gossip."

"Gossip about whom?"

"Oh, no one in particular, David. Washington is Washington. It thrives on scandal. People are always in the wrong beds in Washington, or said to be." There was a tinge of bitterness to that and Cotter thought there had been a quick look at Maggie, and as quickly away. "Somehow I never listen, never remember, because what other people are doing with their lives doesn't interest me."

"And in the last month, since he'd been on the campaign, there wasn't anything your husband told you that would explain why someone wanted to silence him, keep him from talking?"

"David, if you've followed the hearings before the Senator's Committee, you know as much as I do," she said. "All I know is what I saw and heard on television. I know some of the people who have been exposed, indicted. So do you. I know that Mac at one time was working on evidence against some Mafia figure. The crime syndicate? Is that what they call it now to keep it from being ethnic? But what I know, what everyone knows who's followed the hearing, is water over the dam. New

84

cases, new evidence against new people? Mac never talked to me about anything until after it had happened."

Again Cotter detected a faint hint of bitterness in her voice. Mac had been disappointed because she didn't share his interest in sports and gay social parties. But he'd been unwilling to share his work with her, which may have been what interested her.

The study door was flung open with a sort of violence and they all turned to find themselves confronted by the tall, gaunt, gray-haired figure of Ross Crenshaw. The Old Man was still wearing the black glasses he'd had on at the Cathedral, but he'd changed from his funeral cutaway to gray slacks, a gray tweed jacket, a white shirt with a navy blue silk ascot at his neck.

Cotter had never seen the Old Man at close range before, face to face. He might be in shock, as Bill had suggested, but the room seemed to be suddenly charged with an extra electricity. Cotter had felt the same kind of thing in the presence of one or two famous politicians, a few glamorous actors. They seemed larger than life, always, somehow, in Technicolor. When they walked into a room, no one else mattered. Crenshaw, staggered by the tragedy of his son's murder, was still king of the hill, Cotter thought.

"What the hell is going on here?" Crenshaw demanded. His voice had a rasplike edge to it.

Farraday, a former general in the army, a United States Senator, seemed to diminish in size in the presence of the Old Man. He started to explain who Cotter was and why he was here. The black glasses never turned Cotter's way.

"I know who Mr. Cotter is and what he does," Crenshaw interrupted.

"I engaged him a couple of days ago to help us determine who is behind Mac's murder, who used that sick girl to—to—"

"So disengage him," Crenshaw said. "The police, the FBI,

and my people are already on it. Investigators are going to be stumbling over each other."

"I'm afraid I'm in too deep to be called off, Mr. Crenshaw," Cotter said. "One of my people was killed last night."

"That's a police matter," Crenshaw said.

"Not in my world," Cotter said.

For the first time the black glasses were leveled straight at Cotter. "I will not have this case bungled," the Old Man said.

"It seems Mac's office and Maggie's apartment have been gone over by people searching for something Mac had, Father," Gwen said. "David and Maggie came out here thinking someone might try to get at old records Mac has stored here."

"My dear child, be good enough to let people who are trained to handle this kind of thing handle it," Crenshaw said. "There's nothing stored out here anyone could want. All Marcus's important records have been turned over to the special prosecutor."

"Then who was looking for what in his office and in Miss Branson's apartment?" Cotter asked.

"We'll find that out soon enough," the Old Man said. "Meanwhile, Cotter, I ask you to stay out of this. I *tell* you to stay out!" He turned to Maggie. "As long as you're here, Miss Branson, I'd like you to stay. I think you know George Zachery."

Maggie nodded. "He came to the office several times to see your son, Mr. Crenshaw."

"Zachery is head of CrenAm's special security force," the Old Man said, enlightening the rest of them. "He's handling this case for me and I don't want him interfered with by anyone. There may be things Marcus discussed with you, Miss Branson, that could be helpful and that you'll remember when Zachery asks you the right questions. He's on his way out here and should arrive at any time now."

Maggie looked quickly at Cotter. No one else seemed to be

willing to stand up to Crenshaw.

"The FBI let me bring Miss Branson out here with the promise I'd get her back to Washington as quickly as possible," Cotter said.

"I can arrange with the FBI to let her stay here," Crenshaw said. He could influence Presidents, kings, prime ministers and government bureaus.

"This has to do with my part in this," Cotter said. "I had assigned my man Christie to protect Miss Branson after we found someone had her under surveillance. The man who was following her may have been involved with the murder of an FBI agent a couple of weeks ago. Miss Branson is needed in connection with that."

"She's needed here," Crenshaw said, as if that settled that.

Cotter turned to Maggie. "We'd better be going," he said.

"You know if I give the word you can't leave the grounds here, Cotter," the Old Man said.

Cotter smiled a thin, tight smile. "Your army, Mr. Crenshaw? It doesn't seem likely you'll use it with the Senator as a witness."

Crenshaw turned to the Senator with an impatient little gesture. "If you expect my continued support, Lewis, you'll fire this man off the case."

"There's nothing the Senator can fire me from," Cotter said before Farraday could answer. "I was doing him a favor. I wasn't hired. I am my own boss, Mr. Crenshaw." He took Maggie by the arm and led her toward the door.

Crenshaw's face was carved out of rock. "You surely don't believe you can fight a war with me, do you, Mr. Cotter? I promise you you're going to regret what you're doing."

"I can stay, David," Maggie said in a small voice. "I can join you later." She was clearly frightened of Crenshaw.

"No dice," Cotter said. "We've stayed here too long already."

2

Maggie sat very close to Cotter in the front seat of the Mercedes as they drove away from Mac Crenshaw's house and along the highway toward Washington. He could feel her body trembling.

"He won't forgive you for crossing him, David," she said.

"Red Christie's family won't forgive me if I back away," Cotter said. "And I could never forgive myself if I let you out of my sight and anything happened to you."

"Surely I'm not in any danger from the Crenshaws," Maggie said.

He didn't look at her, but that tight smile moved his lips. "Don't use the word 'surely' around this case, love. There's nothing sure about anyone or anything just yet. I'm not saying I think Crenshaw would deliberately harm you. But I am saying that he would use you and wouldn't give a damn what happened to you afterwards. You may be the key to this thing, Maggie, even though you don't know it."

"I don't understand, David. I've told you there's nothing I know that explains anything."

Cotter glanced up into the rear-view mirror. He'd half expected that one of Crenshaw's people might follow them, but there was nothing suspicious behind on the road.

"The reason psychoanalysis is such a long process," he said, "is that it is a business of remembering. You talk and talk, day after day, to the analyst and eventually you remember things that happened to you, maybe when you were five or six years old, that you hadn't known existed. You had ten years with

Mac Crenshaw, professionally and personally. If you and I could hole up somewhere and talk and talk about him, the thing someone thinks you know might pop up out of nowhere. If and when it does, we'll know who to be afraid of and why. Until then you're staying just as close to me as I can keep you."

"Thank you, David," she said in a very small voice.

Traffic moved in a steady stream toward the city. He would keep her close for a much more personal reason, he told himself. He took a quick look down at her. She was staring straight ahead at the road, but she was pressed tight against him. Forever, he thought.

"What do you know about George Zachery?" he asked.

The question took her away from herself. "Not much, except what Mac told me about him. Zachery came to the office one day and Mac said afterwards, 'Would you believe CrenAm has an army and that man is its general?' I was curious. Mac said Zachery was a former CIA agent, and that his job was mostly in the Middle East where CrenAm has oil interests. 'Big corporations, the multinational kind like CrenAm, have armies and spy systems that can match some pretty big countries,' Mac told me. 'With my father's kind of money and power they can overthrow governments, buy secrets, make sure that CrenAm gets and holds exactly what it wants.' I asked him how honest that was, how ethical. He just shrugged and said other corporations and governments use the same methods. 'You fight fire with fire,' Mac said."

"Would you know Zachery if you saw him again?"

"He's not easy to forget," Maggie said. "He's a big man with carrot-red hair and a kind of hungry smile."

"He wasn't the man who followed you, the man outside the bookstore?"

"Lord, no. That one was short, and stocky, and sort of nothing. Except he scared me half to death."

They drove on a mile or two in silence. Their closeness was

all she needed, all he wanted. In the distance the Washington skyline began to emerge.

"What do we do next, David?" she asked.

"We contact Ted Garth to find out if he's learned anything about Arthur Austin's job. After that we disappear, you in particular."

"Disappear where?"

"I haven't thought it through yet," Cotter said. "It depends a little on what Garth has to tell us and whether there is any news waiting at my office from Brownsville."

Ted Garth and another FBI agent named Moss arrived at the Weyland, Cotter's hotel, fifteen minutes after Cotter reached them by phone. The three men sat with Maggie at a corner table in the Weyland's grill room. Neither Maggie nor Cotter had had anything to eat since the night before. There had been no time for breakfast, and it was now almost two-thirty. Maggie had juice, coffee, toast and three strips of crisp bacon. Cotter had a healthy helping of corned beef hash with a poached egg in addition to juice and coffee. The two FBI men, looking like successful young advertising executives, had coffee. The crowded lunch hour was over and only two or three tables in the grill were occupied by a few of the three-hour-for-lunch boys.

Cotter sat facing the entrance to the grill, watching for what Red Christie had described as someone who wanted to be unnoticed and was therefore noticeable.

"Wesley has something that may or may not be helpful to you, David," Garth said.

Wesley Moss was a chain cigarette smoker. His gray eyes seemed constantly narrowed against the smoke. "I was Arthur Austin's contact inside the Bureau," he said. "From what Ted has told me I just may have something. Art was involved with a group of young protesters who call themselves the Scatback's Army."

"The what?"

"Scatback Hughes was a football player. Black. He played for one of the big Southwestern universities and later a couple of years in pro football. The New Orleans Saints it might have been. He was a great open-field runner. Maybe one of the best ever. But he quit about four years ago when the war in Vietnam was still hot and gathered a small army of dissenters around him, black and white, male and female. They marched on Washington; they raised hell at the Republican convention in Miami four years ago. Hughes has been in and out of jail, but there has always been money to defend him. We've never had a good case against him because violence isn't his thing. The Martin Luther King doctrine of nonviolent protest. The Director wanted him so badly he could taste him. He tried to get a morals charge on him because he was moving around the country with a white girl. We never got him, but we were trying. That was Austin's job. The Director thought if the girl was threatened in some way Scatback might blow his cool and turn to something violent. Austin was trying to set him up. He told me that something had been arranged to take place at the Brownsville primaries. Of course that's a couple of weeks away and Art isn't going to be there."

"Unless the assassination of Mac Crenshaw was it," Cotter said.

"Art had been dead for two weeks when that happened."

"And Scatback's girl? Is she missing? Could she have been the assassin?"

Moss shook his head. "She's very much alive. Her name is Patty Prentiss. She and Scatback and a group of what Scatback calls his disciples are in Brownsville now, somewhere up in the hills. They were there the day Mac Crenshaw was killed. Some dotty old lady who believes in peace with a capital P has turned over a farmhouse to them where they're living."

"You've been after them?" Cotter asked.

"Hard," Moss said. "The old lady and a couple of men who work around the place swear that they were all on the farm the afternoon Mac Crenshaw was shot. Like him or not, assassination isn't Scatback's dish. I have to believe that killing Mac Crenshaw isn't something he or his people would plan."

"But they might have killed Austin if they discovered he was an FBI man and not a true disciple?"

"That's the general opinion, but I don't happen to believe it."

"Is there a missing girl disciple?"

"Not that they'll admit," Moss said. "Austin could have told us if he'd lived. But if he had lists of names written down somewhere, we haven't found them. He made written reports to the Bureau about Scatback and Patty Prentiss, but almost nothing about the rest of the group. Scatback and the girl were his targets."

"Then we shouldn't be wasting time with them?" Cotter asked.

Moss lit a cigarette with the stub of one that was almost burning his fingers. "One of Scatback's passionate causes is an outcry against big corporations. They've picketed big oil companies. They chained themselves to the office doors of Quadrant International. I don't think—I know—Scatback wouldn't plan a violence, but some individual, burning up with a fanatical zeal for the cause, might have acted on her own. Mac Crenshaw would represent CrenAm to that kind of a nut. Nothing to do with politics, or Farraday, or primaries."

"But you say Scatback and his people deny that anyone is missing," Cotter said. "Because that girl who shot Mac Crenshaw is missing. She's in the Brownsville morgue."

Moss took a deep drag on his cigarette. "I don't believe

they'd admit someone was missing, if someone is missing. It would bring every cop in New England, the FBI, and Crenshaw's private army down on their necks."

"You tell us all this and at the same time you keep telling us it doesn't lead anywhere," Cotter said.

Moss took a sip of his coffee and found it cold. "Dissenters have been my specialty for the last eight years," he said. "Both the Director and the President seemed a little paranoid on the subject to me. But you do your job as you're ordered to do it. There are all kinds of dissenters: Communists who think they believe in a different system than ours; terrorists who are against any system and mean to blow up the universe to change things; criminals who fake a cause in order to have something to hide behind; idiot kids who get conned into chanting catch phrases and making public spectacles of themselves just for the hell of it; there are what I call political hit men who use dissent as a way to discredit a President, a Senator, a Congressman, a candidate." Moss hesitated. "But then there are genuine dissenters, men and women who are really conscientious objectors to the scheme of things, who detest the violence we call patriotism. I guess some of the early old-time labor leaders belonged in that category. They were called Socialists. That's before we got hipped on Communism. I used to read about Eugene V. Debs in college. There were the militants like John L. Lewis, who fought the exploitation of his coal miners. Then I suppose there was Gandhi, who defeated an empire with nonviolence. Then there was Martin Luther King, who had a dream no one in high places wanted to see come true."

"You should do well on the banquet circuit," Cotter said. He was impatient to get to something that mattered.

"Sorry," Moss said. "I'm trying to say that dissent is my thing. I know the real ones from the fakes, the terrorists from the idealists. Scatback Hughes is a genuine idealist. But in his world you get to know everything about everyone who touches

93

the same base with you. Scatback wouldn't help the FBI, or the CIA, or the Secret Service with anything. He would hide anything from them that could be useful. He might even hide a criminal from them. We in the government services are his mortal enemies. He might, however, help someone who was in real trouble—like you and Miss Branson."

Cotter's laugh was short and mirthless. "Miss Branson, who worked for Mac Crenshaw, the crown prince of CrenAm, and David Cotter, who got into this through Senator Farraday, Ross Crenshaw's candidate for the Presidency. No way your friend Scatback would help us."

Moss glanced at Ted Garth, as though he wanted help.

"I told Wesley," Garth said, "that you didn't give a damn about anything except finding out who killed your friend Christie, and making sure Maggie isn't thrown to the wolves after someone has used her."

Moss leaned forward on his elbows. He looked tired. "Decent people like you and Miss Branson are always being used by somebody," he said. "You're like soldiers in the army; just numbers, expendable. That's what people like Scatback hate about the world. They're just numbers and expendable, like you. He might come up with help if you'd lay it on the line. But don't tell him I said so. That would lead to Katie-bar-the-door. I'm the enemy."

"And am I supposed to pass on anything I learn from Scatback Hughes?"

"I'm not asking you for anything," Moss said. "You see, Cotter, I knew Red Christie. I know his wife and his two kids. You think, before he came to work for you, that he was kicked off the police force because he got too tough with a prisoner?"

"That was his story."

"Do you know who the prisoner was?"

"No."

"He was a man named Zachery, who is a strong-arm boy for

Ross Crenshaw. Crenshaw spoke into the right ears and Christie had had it."

Cotter glanced at Maggie, saw her wide frightened eyes.

"Zachery is in town," Cotter said.

"I know," Moss said. He held up his hand to silence Cotter. "Don't tell me what you're going to do. I couldn't, in my job, keep it a secret."

The twenty-four hours Cotter had given Lester Owen, publisher and editor of the *Capitol Courier* in Brownsville, to produce something useful was up, but there was a message for Cotter at his office to get in touch with Owen when he could. There was also a message from Jack Murphy, the old reporter. It read, as taken down by Cotter's secretary: "Have come across the odor of ripe Limburger cheese. Try me at Hunter's Lodge."

Cotter had taken Maggie directly to his office in downtown Washington when they left the two FBI agents. Cotter's secretary and office manager was a crisp white-haired widow in her middle fifties named Julie Hartman. Her late husband, Joe Hartman, had been a security officer at Dulles Airport, shot to death during an attempted hijacking. She was an extremely efficient, sensitive woman with a passionate hatred for violent men. The minute she laid eyes on Maggie and Cotter she knew that something unusual had happened to her boss. She made no comment. She delivered the two messages from Owen and Murphy and a brief verbal report on what Cotter's operatives were doing.

"Have you seen Betty Christie?" Cotter asked her.

Pity flickered across Julie's nice face. Someone had come to her one night to tell her that her Joe was in the police morgue. Julie had been the message bearer herself to Red Christie's wife.

"Courage, of course," she said. "Although, having been

95

through it myself, I'm not so sure it's really courage. Shock keeps you cool for a while. The crack-up comes later."

"I can't go to see her now," Cotter said, "but watch out for her, Julie. Reassure her about finances if she's worried. When I get back—"

"Where are you going?"

"Brownsville. But if anybody asks you where I am, you haven't any idea."

"You're flying up?"

"Driving. I need my own wheels when I get there."

"How do I get in touch?"

"I won't know till I get there. I'll call you."

"And if you don't?" Julie asked in a flat, cold voice.

"After a couple of days let Senator Farraday know, and have a couple of the boys come looking for me," Cotter said. He felt Maggie's fingers close on his arm. "I don't think we were followed here, Julie, but it's quite possible someone has the office staked out. They'll know Maggie came here with me. If you're asked, admit she was here, but you have no idea where she's gone or what her plans are either."

"Check," Julie said. "It would be nice if you'd take care of yourself, David. It matters to quite a few of us."

Cotter smiled at her. "Taking care of myself is my life's work," he said. He looked down at Maggie. "I have special incentives at the moment."

"So I see," Julie said dryly.

Out in the corridor, waiting for an elevator, Maggie was still clinging to Cotter's arm.

"Does it show, David?" she asked.

"Does what show, love?"

"When we're together, does it—does it show? About us, I mean?"

"I imagine. I mean, how could it not?"

He put his arm around her shoulders and held her close. And

then the elevator door slid open and expressionless faces looked out at them.

Cotter drove the Mercedes to his garage. He transferred Maggie's bags to the fire-engine-red Ferrari. In the trunk was a suitcase of his own. He kept it there permanently, containing a change of clothes, a shaving kit, and a .38 Police Special he was licensed to carry. Maggie settled into the bucket seat on the passenger's side.

"It seems strange not to be telling someone where I'm going," she said.

"Is there someone you should tell?" he asked.

She shook her head. "A girl friend I have dinner with once or twice a week; the office, which really isn't functioning anymore; my hairdresser, with whom I have an appointment tomorrow. It's amazing, but my whole life has been involved with Mac Crenshaw's affairs for years. With Mac gone, it—it's like starting over again in a strange country."

He grinned at her. "I hope you like the looks of it," he said.

The early winter evening was closing in. It would take at least nine hours, weather permitting, to reach Brownsville. The Ferrari made eager noises as Cotter started the motor.

They drove straight through to the outskirts of New York City before they stopped at a neon-lighted roadside place for a chance to freshen up, have a snack, and move on up through New England to Brownsville.

It was after ten when they left New York and just before three in the morning when they found themselves driving along Brownsville's main street. Cotter had hoped to find Hunter's Lodge still open and his friend Jack Murphy propped up at the bar, but it proved to be too late for that. Cotter cruised around, looking for a motel or some kind of tourist house. It was bitter cold outside the warm interior of the Ferrari, probably well below zero, Cotter guessed.

Suddenly there was a flickering light behind them and Cotter glanced up into the rear-view mirror and saw that a State Police car was coming up behind them. There was the usual request for a license.

"What seems to be the problem?" Cotter asked.

"We're curious about all strangers in these parts just now," the trooper said. "This is pretty late at night for cruising around, Mr. Cotter." He handed back Cotter's license. He bent down, peering across Cotter at Maggie.

"We're looking for a place to put up for the night," Cotter said. "I'd hoped Hunter's Lodge might still be open."

"You know Brownsville?" the trooper asked. "Hunter doesn't advertise in any tourist guides."

"I stayed there a couple of nights ago," Cotter said. "If you're worried about me, Officer, I think Captain Shane will vouch for me."

The trooper seemed to relax. "I thought I recognized you," he said. "You were talking to Captain Shane at the barracks a couple of mornings ago. Right?"

"Right."

"There's a pretty good motel about a mile the other side of town," the trooper said. "Follow me. I'll see that you get in."

The trooper car with its blinking lights pulled out ahead of the Ferrari. Cotter's eyes narrowed at the corners. His muscles felt stiff and tired from the long drive.

"You will register as Mrs. Julie Hartman, my secretary," he said to Maggie.

"Why, David?" she asked.

"Someone may be looking for Margaret Branson," he said. "It would be too easy to have your name on the motel register."

The Gateway Motel was like hundreds of others: a main house which apparently contained the office and a restaurant, and a dozen or more small cabin units, built side by side. Cars were parked outside of about eight of the cabins, and there was a VACANCY sign at the front entrance.

The trooper rang some kind of nightbell outside the main house, and after a considerable wait, a sleepy-looking woman wearing a flannel bathrobe and fur-lined bedroom slippers opened the door. She looked relieved at the sight of the trooper.

"Something wrong, Pete?" she asked.

"A couple of customers for you, Mrs. Ramsey," the trooper said. "Friends of Captain Shane's."

"They'll have to come in and sign the register," the woman said.

Cotter and Maggie followed the trooper and Mrs. Ramsey into the house. There was a paneled lounge, decorated with the stuffed heads of deer, a moose, and black bear. Mr. Ramsey was obviously a hunter of some prowess.

Cotter signed his own name and address.

"Mrs. Hartman is my secretary," he said, and turned the register toward Maggie. Her fingers weren't quite steady as she wrote "Mrs. Julie Hartman."

"You got to write down your address, Mrs. Hartman," the woman said.

"Three six Three six Sixteenth Street, North West, Washington, D.C.," Cotter said calmly.

Mrs. Ramsey wrote it in the book. It was actually Julie Hartman's address. "Cabins J and K at the far end of the row of cabins," Mrs. Ramsey said. She produced two keys with lettered tabs attached. "You won't mind if I don't go out with you. Light switch to the right of each door on the inside." She tried to keep it light. "It's colder than a whore's heart out there." She waited for a laugh. It came from the trooper.

Cotter drove the Ferrari to the parking place in front of Cabin J. The trooper followed and actually helped Cotter with the bags. They were conventionally placed, "Mrs. Hartman's" in Cabin J, Cotter's in Cabin K. Cotter thanked the trooper, and asked for his name.

"Stemkowski," the trooper said. "Pete Stemkowski. I'll tell Captain Shane you're back in town when I check in."

"You do that," Cotter said. He stood in the doorway to his cabin, watching the trooper drive away. He glanced at the house in time to see lights go out. He made a small bet with himself that Mrs. Ramsey would be watching from some darkened window to see who slept where. He stepped to the next door and knocked. Maggie must have been standing just inside, waiting. The winter moon turned the snow-covered countryside into a kind of silver daylight.

To hell with Mrs. Ramsey, Cotter told himself, and went into Maggie's cabin.

There is the violence of death and blood in the snow, and three or four days later it stops being the seventh wonder of the world and things get back to normal. At least on the surface.

A dairy truck moved along the town streets, and dogs barked at the milkman who delivered his bottles in a wire carrier from house to house. A gas station and garage opened, and an attendant stretched out a rubber hose by the gas pumps that rang a bell on the inside when a customer drove over it and stopped for refueling. He didn't wait outside for those customers. It was about fifteen below zero that morning, normal for Brownsville. The white-fronted coffee shop down the street was open, and early workers were already drinking steaming coffee with their bacon or ham and eggs. The conversation was casual, about the weather, the skiing conditions at the resort up the mountain, the influx of ski enthusiasts expected for the weekend. Mac Crenshaw was dead and forgotten. The unclaimed body of a girl assassin was still at the local undertaker's, forgotten. At least on the surface.

Below the surface there were carefully concealed tensions. A little after nine o'clock Lester Owen, publisher, owner and editor of the *Capitol Courier,* parked his car in the private area behind the newspaper building and went in the back way to his office. The smell of ink and the rumble of the presses made Owen feel at home. This was where his strength was, where he was top dog, impregnable. He greeted a few employees, who answered in a kind of relieved way. When Les Owen said "good morning," it meant the day was starting on some kind of even keel. And then Owen walked into his glassed-in office and all was not right with the world. Cotter was standing by the far windows, looking out at Brownsville's main street. Owen, scowling, took off his coat and fur hat and hung them on a hat tree in the corner.

"I heard you were back," he said.

Cotter turned. "Oh?" he said.

"I stopped by the trooper barracks to see if there was any news. Shane said you were back in town. Small town, news spreads fast. Everyone talks to everyone."

"I sent a message to Shane that I was here," Cotter said.

"I know." Owen's smile was unpleasant. "Traveling with your secretary," he said. "Attractive girl, according to Pete Stemkowski. Lucky you."

"You phoned me in Washington," Cotter said, not reacting.

"I phoned you because I didn't have anything for you," Owen said. "Twenty-four hours you gave me to dig up something for you. There wasn't anything to find. The troopers haven't found anything. No one around here knows anything about the girl. They brought in those jerk kids from the commune up the mountain. They all swear they never saw that dead broad."

"You're talking about Scatback Hughes?"

"Who else? Black bastard! He makes a half million bucks playing football and then he starts bad-mouthing the country that made it possible. If I was Shane I'd run the whole bunch

101

of them in and keep the heat on them till some one of them broke. It's a cinch they know who that girl is. The FBI thinks they probably killed an agent who'd worked his way into their group, but they've got no proof. Yet, anyway. You put any heat on a black man and you've got half the civil liberty freaks in the country on your back."

"People in Washington who know Hughes and his history don't believe he and his people would have involved themselves in this kind of violence," Cotter said. "That's why the FBI haven't pulled him in. And speaking of motives, Owen, there's one man in your state who must have spent a happy evening after the murder. Your ex-Senator friend, Martin Cleary. Mac Crenshaw exposed him for a bribe-taking crook, ran him out of office. How's that for a motive?"

Owen seemed to swell up as though rage would produce an explosion. "A goddamned frameup from start to finish!" he shouted. "Martin Cleary did more for this state than any man who ever lived here. Cleary was digging into facts about the Crenshaw empire, CrenAm in particular, and they framed him out of his socks."

"Have you asked him, has anyone asked him, if he knows the girl who shot Mac Crenshaw?" Cotter asked.

"So help me God, Cotter, I'm sick of people like you coming into our country and telling us how to run things. So let Ella Marston's friend produce her letter and accuse me. Fred Marston will stand back of me. I'll fight it all the way to the Supreme Court if I have to. But I'm a sonofabitch if I'll let you push me around one day longer."

"It's your funeral," Cotter said. Perhaps he'd pushed a little too hard. After all, there was no letter. He started for the door, but before he reached it, a young man burst in from the outer room.

"I'm sorry to break in, Mr. Owen," the young man said, "but I thought you ought to know."

"What is it, Riley?"

"Fellow who used to work for you," Riley said. "An old newspaper reporter named Jack Murphy. Did you know he was in town?"

"Yes, I knew," Owen said. "Saw him around."

"He was staying at Hunter's Lodge," Riley said. "Someone went to wake him up about half an hour ago and they found him beaten half to death. They've taken him to the hospital but they don't think he's going to make it. I wondered how you wanted it handled. I mean, since he used to work here."

Owen seemed to get himself back into control. "He was a drunk but a hell of a newspaperman, Riley. We go all out for him. Paper will offer a reward. Stay with it."

Riley turned and ran out of the office. Owen looked at Cotter. "Your friends don't seem to be very lucky lately, do they, Cotter? Jack Murphy was your friend, wasn't he? Want to go see what happened to him?"

What happened to Murphy was fairly simple. Hunter's Lodge wasn't a hotel, just a restaurant and bar. There were three or four bedrooms on the second floor of what had once been a private home on Brownsville's main street. Sometimes a good customer who came from somewhere out in the country would take on a little too much at the bar and Warren Hunter would bed him down rather than risk letting him drive home potted. Jack Murphy had been on a five-day bender and Hunter, out of the goodness of his heart and an old-time friendship, had let him stay at the lodge. But there was no service in the room, no key for the door lock. Each night for five days Hunter had put Murphy to bed with a bottle of booze. Each morning he had waked him, got him headed for the bathroom and a shower and the start of a new day. This morning he had gone to wake his friend and found him savagely beaten. At first he thought Murphy was dead, but he found a faint pulse, phoned for the ambulance, and so far that was that.

Captain Shane was in charge.

The State Trooper captain and Warren Hunter were New England born and bred, spoke the same language, had a matching respect for people who got somewhere by hard work. Shane would have been a better cop if he hadn't had sympathy for human frailty. Young men who drink too much are a pain in the neck because they tend to make rowdy troubles or wrap themselves around trees in car accidents. Old men who drink too much Shane felt sympathy for because life had passed them by, they had noplace to go but the immediate present. Jack Murphy was in that category, plus the fact that he went about the business of final self-destruction with a kind of humor. Shane had liked him for that.

Selling liquor to all types and kinds of people was Warren Hunter's business. But he ran the lodge by certain rigid rules. When, in his judgment, someone had had enough, Warren Hunter wouldn't sell that customer another drink for love or money. Under-age kids couldn't buy a warm beer from him. But there were one or two old-timers, like old John Connors who lived in isolation with a shrewish wife in the valley, who would come to the lodge to blot out time for a while. Hunter would let him go as far as he wanted, put him to bed when the time came, having demanded old John's car keys before the drinking started. Jack Murphy was in the same category, privileged to drink himself blind if he chose.

On this morning both Shane and Hunter were outraged by what had happened to "a harmless old coot."

"Anyone else spend the night here?" Shane asked Hunter.

"No," Hunter said. "That is, except Tommy Carmichael and myself. Tommy has a room over the kitchen in the other wing. But I saw Murphy alive and well—as well as he could be

104

—long after Tommy was downstairs and doing the morning chores."

Tommy Carmichael was a jack-of-all-trades for Hunter, dishwasher, handyman, night watchman, resident plumber and carpenter.

"You saw Murphy this morning before someone got to him?" Shane asked.

Hunter nodded. "Around six A.M.," he said.

"Like take it from the top, will you, Warren?"

"Murphy's been on a real tear ever since the shooting," Hunter said. "He was standing close enough to Crenshaw when it happened to imagine he could have been splattered with Crenshaw's blood and brains. He's been trying to wipe his clothes clean for five whole days. Shook up, he was, bad." Hunter shrugged. "He's an old friend. Better he should bomb out here, where I could keep an eye on him, than I should kick him out into the night. He'd only start drinking white lightning out of somebody's silo."

"Good friends are hard to come by these days," Shane said. "About this morning."

"It really begins with last night," Hunter said. "Murphy had started in late yesterday morning—like every morning the last five days. But along about suppertime he changed his pattern.

" 'It may blow your mind, Warren-baby,' he said to me, 'but I yearn for food.'

"It did surprise me because he's one that never eats anything when he's drinking. He ordered a steak sandwich with some tomato juice spiked with Worcestershire sauce and Tabasco. He ate like a man taking medicine and then he called me over.

" 'Warren-baby, I'm a man trying with all his might to build character. It might turn out that tomorrow will be the most important day of my life. I've got to be in shape for it. But just in case I don't have the stamina to hold out, I'd like a bottle to take to my room, along with your prayers for my ability to turn my back on temptation. And be good enough to call me around nine o'clock.'

"He'd taken a bottle to his room every one of the previous four nights and every morning it was empty. So I didn't pay much attention, give it much thought. Except he went up to bed about nine o'clock instead of when the bar closed at two.

"My routine is to get up around six o'clock to see that the morning chores get started; coffee urns washed and started up for opening time, cleanup under way. That's Tommy and Mrs. Hamner from next door. On my way downstairs I looked in on Murphy, wondering how well he'd resisted temptation. You could have knocked me over with a feather when I saw that bottle of whiskey, unopened on the bureau. Murphy had made it, and he was sleeping like a baby."

"That was at six o'clock?" Shane asked.

"I set my alarm for six. I'd been to the john, washed my face, put on some clothes. It could have been ten after. You move kind of quick in the morning because there's no heat upstairs until I get down to the main floor and turn up the thermostat. Probably less than ten minutes."

"So go on."

"I'm downstairs. I make breakfast for myself and Tommy and Mrs. Hamner. Coffee, eggs, juice, English muffins. For the next three hours the three of us were doing our regular chores. No one was out of sight of anyone else for—for long enough. I notice from the bar clock that it's a few minutes after nine, and I remember I'd promised to call Murphy for what he thought might turn out to be the most important day of his life."

"He never told you what was going to be so important about it?"

"No. Just kind of a sly smile, like a man with a big secret."

106

"So you went upstairs to wake him."

A nerve twitched in Hunter's cheek. His tongue emerged to moisten dry lips. "Yeah, I went up," he said.

"And you saw him like the ambulance people found him?"

Hunter nodded.

"I need the details, Warren."

"I know," Hunter said, "I know." He fumbled in his shirt pocket for a cigarette. "I remember from the war what blood smells like. Kind of sickly sweet if there's a lot of it. And there was a lot of it."

"Murphy put up quite a fight," Shane suggested.

"No fight at all, the way I saw it," Hunter said. "Everything in the room was perfectly neat, untouched, that whiskey bottle just where I'd seen it before on the bureau. Only the bed was messed up, looking like Murphy had taken a bath in blood. I went over to him. His face was lopsided, knocked out of shape. He must have a broken jaw. Teeth smashed in and broken. And his head you wouldn't believe, his white hair turned the color of claret wine. It looked like someone had moved up alongside the bed while Murphy was asleep and flailed at him with something—a piece of pipe, a crowbar, a jack handle or a big wrench of some sort."

"But you didn't see anything like that?"

"Not then, not later," Hunter said. "I was sure Murphy was dead, but I remembered my war training. I felt for a sign of a pulse, in his throat like they taught us. There was something. Just a flicker, but something. So I ran to the phone, called the ambulance and then you."

"Now we come to the important part, Warren," Shane said.

"I know. Who did it," Hunter said. "How did he get in without me, or Mrs. Hamner, or Tommy knowing? Didn't we hear any sounds from that savage beating? How did he get out?"

"That's it," Shane said.

"There was nobody here when we closed up last night," Hunter said.

"Did you search the place?"

"Well, not as though we were looking for anyone hiding. I mean, we looked to make sure no one had fallen asleep in the ladies' or the men's. We locked all the doors, put the place to bed like always. I know all the customers who were here at closing time left. I'd swear there were no strangers around all evening."

"It didn't have to be a stranger," Shane said. "Can you remember who was here all night—I mean while you were open?"

"I could probably dredge it up, perhaps with help from a few others."

"No doors were forced while you were asleep? You, and Tommy Carmichael in his room, and Murphy in his?"

"No doors have been forced then or any other time."

"But it's not impossible that someone could have hidden somewhere when you closed, and gotten to Murphy after you were all asleep."

"Why would he wait until after we were all awake again and going about our morning chores? Remember, Murphy was okay a little after six this morning. He could have done it while we were asleep and just let himself out. It doesn't make sense he was hidden here all night."

"How could he have got in this morning, after you were all up?" Shane asked.

"I've thought about it," Hunter said. "There are a lot of trash bags to take out in the morning. We put them in garbage cans back of the building for the sanitation service to pick up. That's Tommy's job. He carries them out the back door, and he leaves that back door unlocked. That's routine. Once he unlocks the door, he has no reason to lock it again till the next night."

"So the man we want could have come in that unlocked door while you were all working in the front of the house, slipped upstairs and clobbered Murphy, and let himself out the way he got in?"

"It could be," Hunter said.

"And nobody saw or heard him?"

"None of us; not me, or Tommy, or Mrs. Hamner. It was daylight outside. Somebody could have seen someone hanging around or walking away."

That was Hunter's statement, later taped, transcribed, and signed by him. Cotter saw it without very much resistance from Captain Shane because he had something to trade for it. "Have come across the odor of ripe Limburger cheese." Murphy's message to Cotter in Washington. Murphy must have assumed Cotter would come to Brownsville to smell for himself. That may have accounted for his expectation that today might be the most important day of his life.

"I remember you said he was grateful to you, Mr. Cotter," Shane said. "How was it? You convinced him he hadn't been an accessory to Mac Crenshaw's murder?"

"That's how it was. He'd agreed to keep an eye on things for me here while I went back to Washington to try to pick up some kind of lead there."

"And did you?"

"Yes and no," Cotter said. "Friends of mine in the FBI were thinking about Scatback Hughes and his people who are located somewhere near here."

"First thing we thought of," Shane said. "But the agents up here didn't buy it, and we had no evidence at all. Your friends think differently?"

"Not that Hughes was involved directly with the killing, but that he might know something which he wouldn't tell to the law. They thought I might be able to persuade him to tell me things he wouldn't tell to the cops."

"I doubt it," Shane said. "What was Murphy doing for you?"

"Keeping his eyes and ears open for me. The message implies he stumbled onto something. Someone made sure he didn't pass it on to me. What are his chances?"

Shane shrugged. "He's critical, in intensive care. They don't give him much chance."

"And he hasn't talked?"

"God, no. If you'd seen him, you wouldn't ask."

"I'm going to see him," Cotter said. "I'd like to go through his belongings. There might be something, some kind of hint or clue."

"There was nothing at Hunter's Lodge," Shane said. "Hunter supplied him with a razor and a toothbrush. Just the clothes he was wearing, an overcoat, a hat. A wallet with his driver's license, about fifty dollars in cash, a telephone number on a scrap of paper which turns out to be your Washington office." Shane handed him a couple of sheets of paper across his desk. "You care to see these? Statements from Tommy Carmichael and Mrs. Hamner."

Cotter read through them quickly.

STATEMENT FROM MRS. STEPHEN HAMNER:

I reported to work about twenty minutes past six, the usual time. Warren [Hunter] was making coffee like always. Tommy [Carmichael] was washing glasses behind the bar. It was no different than any other day. It was like always until a little after nine o'clock when Warren went upstairs to wake up Jack Murphy. "Murphy asked me to call him about nine o'clock," Warren said. "I almost forgot." A few minutes later he came running down the stairs, looking like death. "Someone's tried to kill Murphy!" he shouted at us and went to the phone. That's all I know.

QUESTION: Did you notice any blood on Hunter's clothes when he came downstairs? [The interrogating officer had a theory that Hunter might have bludgeoned Murphy when he went upstairs.]

ANSWER: You crazy? Murphy was Warren's friend.

QUESTION: Did you hear anyone moving around when you were at work? Did you hear a door slam, anything unusual?

ANSWER: I tell you it was like any other day till Warren went upstairs and found him.

(Signed) Nellie Hamner.

The other was a little longer.

STATEMENT FROM THOMAS CARMICHAEL:

There wasn't anything any different from any morning. Warren [Hunter] and I both got downstairs a little after six. I did what I always do, started cleaning up the back bar and getting last night's trash in plastic bags. Warren was making coffee. Nellie [Mrs. Stephen Hamner] came in before six-thirty. That's when she's due, six-thirty, but she always comes in a little earlier. It was like always. Warren made breakfast and we knocked off to eat it. Then I took out the plastic bags of trash and put them in the metal cans at the back. Everything was like always. It wasn't till Warren went upstairs after nine o'clock and found Murphy that anything was unusual. After that all hell broke loose—the ambulance, the troopers.

QUESTION: Let's go back to the night before, Tommy. You and Hunter closed up as usual. How does that go?

ANSWER: Warren checks out the johns to make sure no

one's passed out there, or fallen asleep sitting on the can. Then he locks up the front. I go back to the kitchen and make sure all the stove burners are turned off. Then I lock the back door.

QUESTION: You have a key to lock it?

ANSWER: It's a Yale lock. You just release the catch and slam it shut. Then there's a safety bar that fits into place. Same on the front door.

QUESTION: So that if somebody could pick the lock there'd still be the safety bars to contend with?

ANSWER: You'd have to smash them open and you could hear them all over the house if that happened.

QUESTION: You're sure the back door was locked and the bar in place?

ANSWER: Sure I'm sure.

QUESTION: And in the morning nothing was out of order?

ANSWER: You mean did anyone break in the back way, the answer is no.

QUESTION: So you and Hunter went to bed after locking up. Did you hear anything unusual during the night?

ANSWER: My room is in the other wing of the house from where Murphy and Warren were sleeping. It would have to be very loud for me to hear anything because when I sleep I sleep.

QUESTION: So the next morning everything was like it should be?

ANSWER: As far as I know. I know now that Warren looked in on Murphy on his way downstairs and that he was all right then. At the time he didn't mention it. No reason to, I suppose. After twenty years in this business talking about drunks gets to be a bore. They aren't funny and they aren't very interesting. Murphy was a nice guy, but he was far-out gone.

QUESTION: So after breakfast you took the safety bar off

the back door and fastened back the lock catch so you could carry out the bags of trash. It snowed a little toward early morning. You see any fresh footprints out there?

ANSWER: I didn't notice anything.

QUESTION: If anyone came in from the outside after you'd unlocked the back door, wouldn't they leave wet footprints inside the kitchen?

ANSWER: I suppose they would. Only I was in and out about half a dozen times with bags of trash. If I saw any wet footprints, I'd of thought they were mine, I guess. Hell, I had no reason to wonder about anything like that till after whoever it was was long gone.

QUESTION: You didn't notice any blood on Warren Hunter's clothes when he came downstairs after finding Murphy?

ANSWER: Christ, no! What are you getting at, anyway?

(Signed) Thomas Carmichael.

There was a note to the effect that the questioning officer was Trooper Stemkowski, Cotter's friend of the night before.

Cotter handed back the statements. "Your man Stemkowski seemed to be hipped on the possibility that Hunter may have attacked Murphy."

"When there's no way for anyone to get in a place, you have to consider the people who are already in," Shane said. "I don't think Warren did it, but you have to consider it. The only other possibility is that someone came in the back door after Carmichael had unlocked it and gone to work in the front of the house."

"Someone familiar with the place, the morning habits, and exactly where to look for Murphy," Cotter said.

"You have to think maybe," Shane said.

"Someone local," Cotter persisted. "I wouldn't have known about the back door routine or where to look for Murphy."

113

"You got something there," Shane said. "Whoever it was had to know Murphy was sleeping at the Lodge. That wasn't his regular place to stay."

"But you don't know where that regular place was?"

"Will know before too long," Shane said. "We're asking around."

"Hunter doesn't know?"

"He says not. There aren't too many possibilities right in town, and Murphy didn't have a car so he wouldn't be staying in any of the fancy motels the skiers use. They're mostly outside walking distance in winter. In town a few old ladies rent rooms. They don't like accommodating drunks, and Murphy is notorious."

Cotter stood up. "I'm going to the hospital," he said. "Can I check back with you in case anything new turns up?"

"Sure thing," Shane said. "And you'll return the favor?"

"Glad to," Cotter said.

Inside an oxygen tent at the Brownsville Hospital's intensive care unit Jack Murphy looked like an entombed mummy. His head, face, and neck were bandaged so that only his eyes were visible. His arms and hands were bandaged and in splints, suspended by an apparatus that held them up and away from his body. A sheet was tented over the rest of his body so that Cotter couldn't see what other damage there might be.

The doctor, named Miller, had only been willing to take Cotter into the unit after he'd checked back with Captain Shane.

"Worst beating I ever saw a man take and live," Dr. Miller said. "Skull fracture, God knows how bad; both arms broken in several places; ribs smashed; jaw broken. Murphy must have been like the famous old Russian villain, Rasputin. He just wouldn't die! There must be someone around somewhere who

114

can't believe the news he's getting. He can't believe that Murphy isn't dead."

"And will he die?" Cotter asked.

Dr. Miller shrugged. "He should be dead now," he said. "But when you've practiced medicine as long as I have, you get to believe in miracles. This man doesn't want to die, that's for sure. And that gives him a chance."

"Any chance he'll be able to communicate?" Cotter asked. "Because he knows why this happened to him."

"God, Mr. Cotter, he can't even blink his eyelids. If he lives, it'll be some time before we can find out what still works. I'm talking about days, maybe even weeks, not hours."

"Can anybody get at him here? Because whoever did this to him can't risk his living," Cotter said.

Dr. Miller looked as if he couldn't believe what he heard. "Are you saying you believe someone might—"

"That's what I believe," Cotter said.

From a phone booth in the hospital lobby Cotter called the Gateway Motel. Somebody answered and he asked to be connected with Cabin J. He glanced at his watch as he waited. He had left Maggie, sleeping peacefully, at about seven-thirty. He had left a note for her saying he was going to have a look around Brownsville, back around nine. He'd been gone a couple of hours longer than he'd expected.

No one answered the phone in Cabin J.

Presently the female voice on the switchboard told him what he knew. No answer. He asked to speak to Mrs. Ramsey. After another long wait during which Cotter imagined his body was freezing, the voice of the proprietress came on. Cotter identified himself and said there must be something wrong with the phone in Cabin J. He was trying to reach his secretary, Mrs. Hartman. It was important. Would Mrs. Ramsey please—

"Oh, she took off about half, three-quarters of an hour ago," Mrs. Ramsey said cheerfully.

"Took off? You mean she checked out?"

"Oh, no."

"Then what do you mean?" Cotter's voice was harsh.

"Why, a man came, knocked on the door of Cabin J. I thought at first, just looking casually out the window, it was you, Mr. Cotter. Then I saw his car was black and remembered yours is red and foreign. This man knocked on the door of Cabin J and your Mrs. Hartman opened it. The man just stood there talking. She seemed to know him, I'd say."

"Can you describe him, Mrs. Ramsey?"

"Not really. He was wearing a tan parka with the hood pulled up, so I couldn't see his face. Mrs. Hartman went back into the cabin and closed the door. The man waited outside. Then she came out again, dressed to go somewhere. She and the man went off together in his car."

The sun was bright on the Brownsville snow. To Cotter, running across the hospital parking lot to the red Ferrari, the brightness itself was somehow threatening. He drove like a lunatic, skidding through turns, away from the hospital and out the north road toward the Gateway. He didn't stop at the main house, but stormed onto the front of Cabin J. The door was unlocked.

Inside the place seemed to be in a comfortable disorder. The bed in which he and Maggie had slept was still unmade. Maggie's personal things were in the closet where she'd hung them, and brush, comb, and cosmetics were on the dressing table in front of the mirror. Cotter saw his own reflection in the mirror and wondered, for a startled moment, who it was.

He looked everywhere for a written message. He couldn't find one if it had been left. He stood in the center of the room, his heart like a thumping cold stone in his chest. Maggie wouldn't have gone off with someone she didn't know, wouldn't have gone without leaving word for him. Not voluntarily.

"She seemed to know him," Mrs. Ramsey had said.

Or she believed what she was told. Nothing would have persuaded her to go anywhere, after explicit instructions, unless the man in the parka had convinced her he had a message from Cotter. She'd have left a message unless she thought she was being taken to some place Cotter was waiting for her.

Cotter turned and pounded both fists against the wall of the cabin.

Part Three

The Moves to Checkmate

1

Cotter slammed the Ferrari around and headed for the main house and the lobby with its stuffed animal heads. Mrs. Ramsey was behind the desk, her mouth and eyes made up to look like a 1930s Joan Crawford. It wasn't a successful venture.

The lady was smiling as Cotter came through the front door, but the smile froze at the sight of his face.

"Everything all explained?" she asked, forcing something that was meant to be cheerful.

"Nothing is explained," Cotter said. He pressed his hands down hard on the reception desk and leaned forward so that his face wasn't more than a foot from Mrs. Ramsey's. "You say you can't describe the man, Mrs. Ramsey?"

"It's a hundred yards from here to Cabin J!" she protested. It was a frightened whine. "I told you on the phone, Mr. Cotter, he was wearing a parka with the hood pulled up."

"Was he tall, short and fat?"

"Well, about like you, I'd guess. Tallish."

"The car. Can you tell me more about it?"

"Black, like I told you. Not a compact, I'd say. A medium-sized car."

"The license?"

"My God, Mr. Cotter, that cabin is a hundred yards away!"

"But when they drove out they came back past the house here?"

"They didn't. They went out the far end of the parking space."

Cotter tried to control a scalding fear for Maggie. It wasn't helping to frighten this vain, stupid woman. He lowered his voice. "In this business you must notice license plates, Mrs. Ramsey. It would be a sort of an automatic, I should think."

"But the car was a hundred yards away!"

"I don't expect you to have seen the numbers," he said. "But was it an in-state or out-of-state plate? The colors?"

"The car was headed in toward the cabin when I first saw it," the woman said. "You couldn't see the plates."

"And when it left?"

"I just plain didn't notice. I saw your secretary get in the car with the man and they drove off."

"Did he force her in, Mrs. Ramsey?"

"No! At least no way I could see he did. He got in his side, she walked around and got in the passenger side."

Cotter straightened up and his lungs felt constricted as he tried to draw in a deep breath. "Has anyone inquired for me or Mrs. Hartman here at the desk?" he asked.

"Not that I know of, Mr. Cotter."

"Would there be a record of any incoming phone calls for us since seven o'clock this morning? That's when I left."

"There aren't any messages," the woman said, glancing at what were key boxes behind her.

"Who answers the phone beside you, Mrs. Ramsey?"

"Betty or I, whoever's closest." She gestured toward a young girl who was trying hard to look as though she wasn't listening. "Were there any calls for Cabin J, Betty?"

"Only the one from Mr. Cotter himself a little while back," the girl said.

"No one called to ask where Mrs. Hartman or I were staying?" Cotter asked.

"No, sir," the girl said.

"And the man in the car," Cotter said, "did he stop to ask which cabins we had?"

"He didn't stop at all," Mrs. Ramsey said. "I—I didn't see him until just when he pulled up outside Cabin J. I was curious, so I watched."

"How could he know that was where to go?" Cotter asked. That was the key question.

"Well, if he saw your car parked there earlier," the woman said. "Your car is kind of noticeable, Mr. Cotter."

"If there are messages, be sure to keep them carefully," Cotter said. "I'll keep checking back with you."

"I hope it's nothing serious, Mr. Cotter."

Serious!

Cotter walked out to his car and got in; he sat gripping the wheel so hard his hands ached. He didn't start the motor because he didn't have the remotest idea where to go. For the first time in his career as an investigator he found deep and passionate and very personal emotions getting in his way. Maggie, so newly everything to him!

He tried to blot out fear and get his professional mind to working. Back in Washington there were people who knew or guessed that Maggie was with him. Julie Hartman knew they had gone to Brownsville, but nothing on God's earth would force her to tell anyone. But others might guess easily enough. There was one thing no one in Washington could know or guess. No one could know where they were staying. They hadn't known themselves until they'd arrived in Brownsville. Julie hadn't known, nor Garth and Moss, the two FBI agents, nor Senator Farraday, nor any of the Crenshaws. No one in Brownsville had known in advance. Murphy might have hoped Cotter would reply to his message by coming, Lester Owen

123

might have thought he would come, but there was no way they could know where he and Maggie would stay. And then it fell neatly into place. Trooper Stemkowski knew where they were staying. He had brought them here, checked them in, helped them with Maggie's luggage at Cabin J. He had announced he would tell Shane. There was no reason for him to keep what he knew a secret from anyone who might ask.

The Ferrari's engine roared to life, and the red car hurtled out of the Gateway yard and down the highway toward the trooper barracks.

Stemkowski was off duty, and Shane was out somewhere on the Murphy case. Cotter managed to pry Stemkowski's home location from the desk sergeant. He lived with a fairly recent bride in a cottage south of town on Route 179.

Ten minutes later Cotter was knocking at the door of the trooper's home. A pleasant-faced girl wearing a checkered kitchen apron over a blue cotton dress opened the door.

"My husband's asleep," she told Cotter. "He had the night shift, and then he worked way overtime on the thing that happened at Hunter's Lodge. Could you come back later?"

"It's very important that I talk to him," Cotter said.

She sensed his urgency and invited him in. He found himself in a warm kitchen. Something from his childhood assailed him —the fragrance of freshly baked bread. He saw three loaves, still in their oven pans on a side table. Mrs. Stemkowski must have just taken them out of the oven as he knocked on her door.

The girl went up a narrow flight of stairs to the second floor and Cotter could hear the murmur of voices, but not what they said. Then she came back down the stairs.

"Pete said would you go up to his room. It's the first door on the right."

Cotter went up. The bedroom, a window open, was cold. Stemkowski lay in bed under a patchwork eiderdown. He had lighted a cigarette and his exposed arm was bare.

"There has to be sometime in this life when you can sleep," the trooper said. He wasn't pleased by Cotter's presence. "What's up and why couldn't it wait?"

Cotter told him. He still talked about "Mrs. Hartman, my secretary." "She wouldn't have gone away with anyone unless she thought I'd sent for her. The man who took her knew exactly where to find her. You are the only person who knew where we were, what cabins we had."

"The town is full of outside cops, FBI people," Stemkowski said. "They may have wanted to question her about something."

"But they had to know where to find her," Cotter said. "You are the only person who knew. Who did you tell?"

Stemkowski stared at the smoke that curled up from his cigarette. "Mind closing the window?" he asked. "It's colder than hell in here."

Cotter closed the window. Stemkowski sat up in bed and pulled the eiderdown around his muscular shoulders and chest.

"You think something bad has happened to her?" he asked.

"Somebody faked her right out of her shoes," Cotter said. "She'd never have left unless she thought I'd sent for her. Who knew, Stemkowski?"

"I told Shane. You mentioned him. You said he could vouch for you. I told him you and your secretary were holed up at the Gateway."

"You told him which cabins?"

"God, Mr. Cotter, I don't remember. No reason why I should have. No reason why I shouldn't. I know he didn't ask." He reached out and crushed his cigarette in a saucer on the bedside table. "I was on patrol till eight o'clock. Midnight to eight A.M. was my shift. I saw him a little after eight. I was still making out my reports when we got the call from Hunter's Lodge. Man named Murphy was badly beaten up."

"I know. I know Murphy. Shane showed me your interrogations of Carmichael and Mrs. Hamner."

"Then he must trust you."

"Did anybody else ask you about me or Mrs. Hartman?"

Stemkowski snapped his fingers. "Yes, by God, there was someone, now that I think about it. A reporter named Riley from the *Capitol Courier*. He was driving me crazy with questions. I was trying to get out of the Lodge to get to the barracks to help with the interrogations. He saw you. You were there in the bar with Les Owen, Riley's boss. He asked me if you were David Cotter. He wanted to know what you were doing there. I was trying to shake him. I said he should ask you himself, that you were staying at the Gateway."

"But you didn't tell him what cabins we had?"

"Why should I? I was just trying to get rid of him."

Cotter knew that Riley had already seen him in Owen's office when he'd come to report the Murphy beating and to ask how to handle the story. That was before he and Owen had gone to Hunter's Lodge. But the reporter hadn't been introduced at that time. His curiosity could have had no more significance except that Riley was a good reporter covering every angle of his story. It could have been much more than that.

One thing was certain. There was a great deal more going on behind the scenes than a one-man operation. Farraday's "man behind the gun" was some kind of conspiracy that involved the stocky man outside the Washington bookstore with the dead FBI agent's papers; whoever had killed that agent; whoever had murdered Red Christie; whoever had tried to murder Jack Murphy; and now, whoever had lured Maggie out of Cabin J. Crisscrossing in the background were the State Police and the FBI, Crenshaw's private army headed by George Zachery, and Cotter himself. Cotter had had Murphy in Brownsville, set up to report anything he saw or heard.

Someone else could have had Riley, a young reporter on the only daily newspaper in the state, prepared to report anything he saw or heard. Riley would almost certainly try to stay on the good side of the State Police or the FBI. It was a way to exclusive stories. But he could also have taken an extra dollar to report to someone else. "If Cotter shows up, let us know." Cotter, by the simple fact that he was nosing around for truth, was dangerous to someone—so dangerous that Murphy had to be eliminated to keep from reporting on his "Limburger cheese."

There had been time, after Riley had confirmed through Stemkowski that the man with his boss was Cotter, to phone whoever it was who was paying that extra buck and report that Cotter was in town and staying at the Gateway. Cotter had spent almost two hours talking to Shane, listening to and reading the reports on Murphy's beating, before he'd headed back for Maggie. Plenty of time for the man in the parka to go to Cabin J and flimflam Maggie. How would he know that Maggie was there? People in Washington could have reported that Cotter was traveling with Maggie, that "Mrs. Hartman" was really Margaret Branson. Margaret Branson could be even more dangerous to them than Cotter.

Cotter looked at Stemkowski, who had gotten out of bed and was pulling on some clothes. Stemkowski could be on someone's payroll. Shane could be on someone's payroll. There wasn't a soul in this Godforsaken, frozen town who could be trusted. Lester Owen was surely on the side of the enemy. Cotter suddenly realized that in Brownsville he couldn't ask for directions to the men's room without someone who was interested in him knowing where he was going.

"You want me to report Mrs. Hartman missing?" Stemkowski asked. He was sitting on the edge of the bed, pulling on his boots.

"It would be a relief to know where she is," Cotter said.

There was, he supposed, an outside chance that someone was honest. But who?

Back in his car Cotter drove slowly along the highway toward town. He drove slowly because he was headed nowhere. Where to go? Where to look and what to look for? Maggie could have been taken hundreds of miles away from here by now. Or dropped through a fishing hole in the ice of the river that wound along the highway and through the town. This was the river in which a woman named Ella Marston had drowned herself rather than submit to Lester Owen's sexual sadisms.

You grow hot and cold by turns in a situation like this, Cotter knew. Hot with rage and the unbearable need for a violent confrontation, cold with anxiety and fear for someone else, not for yourself.

Who could possibly give him help in this town? Warren Hunter had been Murphy's friend, but Hunter's livelihood depended on the goodwill of the Brownsville authorities. Would he help a stranger, even on behalf of his friend Murphy? Cotter doubted it.

It finally dawned on him that there was someone in the area who might be persuaded to help, who was certainly not on the side of the assassins, the cops, the CrenAm people. He found himself thinking of Scatback Hughes and his disciples, living on a farm "somewhere up in the hills" under the protection of some "dotty old woman." Wesley Moss, the FBI man in Washington, had suggested the former football star might be the way to some kind of truth about the savagery that had engulfed Arthur Austin, Mac Crenshaw, Red Christie, and now Jack Murphy. Ice in his veins reminded Cotter that he might have to add Maggie to that list.

It was absurd, but Cotter felt he couldn't stop someone on Main Street and ask them where the commune was. Everyone

128

in Brownsville must know. But if he asked the wrong person, someone might be warned off, someone prepared.

"Somewhere up in the hills" meant to the north of town. The mountains, glittering with snow and ice and splashed with the dark green of pine and fir trees, were there. Up there was a farm, and a dotty old woman, and a couple of dozen young people dedicated to peace and decency and marked down as Communists and possible traitors. With them, though, might be one answer, one lead that would take Cotter in the direction of Maggie. The man behind the gun was more, now, than the person who had persuaded a crazed girl to eliminate Mac Crenshaw; he was the person responsible for Maggie's abduction. For that's what it was, an abduction, and Cotter knew that if he found him he would be no less ready to destroy him inch by inch than Ross Crenshaw was.

He headed the Ferrari north. He was alert now to the possibility of being followed, but he saw nothing in his mirrors to suggest that anyone was on his tail. The roads climbing up into the hills were well plowed and sanded. He remembered that winter skiers would be crowding in over the weekend, probably beginning tomorrow night, a Friday. Winter sportsmen were important to the area's economy, and the roads were well prepared for them.

As the red car climbed upward, houses became farther and farther apart. Most of them had barn complexes nearby that suggested they were small farms owned by "natives," and not renovated vacation homes of city people. Cotter had no way of knowing whether he was on target or not. Finally he approached a small white clapboard house with smoke pouring out of a fieldstone chimney. A brown collie dog barked with a kind of sham fierceness as Cotter pulled over to the side of the road. Just outside the back door of the house a large fat man was chopping firewood on a wooden block. As Cotter got out of his car, the woodchopper, ax in hand, came toward him. Cotter was astonished. It wasn't a man at all, but a large fat woman.

"Can I help you?" the woman asked. There was a flat, New England tone to the voice, but educated-sounding.

Cotter glanced at a white mailbox with the name DUMPHY painted on it in black letters.

"My name is Cotter," he said.

Nothing happened to the round, pleasant face, flushed from the cold. His name didn't seem to register anything.

"I've fallen in love with your countryside," he said.

"You looking for someplace, Mr. Cotter?"

"That's exactly it," he said. "I don't trust real estate agents. They're always trying to sell you what you don't want and not showing you what you want to see."

"You looking to buy something?" the woman asked.

"If I see the right thing," Cotter said.

"Nothing I know of around these parts is for sale," the woman said.

"Sometimes people can be persuaded. This is a charming house."

"Belonged to my grandfather before me," the woman said. "Not for sale now or ever."

"I knew I couldn't be that lucky," Cotter said. "I envy you —is it Mrs. Dumphy?"

The woman smiled. "Nowadays we say Miz. But I'm old enough now it doesn't matter you should know it's Mrs. Dumphy."

The collie dog, having decided about Cotter, nuzzled up to him and Cotter scratched his head. "One thing I was concerned about while I was looking," he said, "was that I wasn't too anxious to locate near this hippie commune I hear about in town."

Mrs. Dumphy froze. "Well, you don't have to worry about

130

that, mister, because there's nothing for sale around here." She turned back toward her woodpile.

"You mean the commune is around here somewhere, Mrs. Dumphy?"

"My farm just up the road," Mrs. Dumphy said. "And if you don't like it, mister, you can lump it."

Cotter let his breath out in a long sigh. For the first time in several days the gods were on his side.

He edged the Ferrari on up the hill road, snowbanks high on each side of it. There was almost a hairpin left just above Mrs. Dumphy's house and there, with a view down the valley that would have been breathtaking had he been in the mood for it, Cotter came on the farm. There was a big old house, needing a coat of paint, and a collection of red barns and outbuildings, a silo. There were a few head of black and white cattle and an ancient-looking bay horse in a fenced-in paddock, nibbling at hay that had been placed there on the snow. Some noisy Plymouth Rock chickens announced Cotter's arrival in the yard. As he got out of the car, he saw that Mrs. Dumphy's collie dog had followed the Ferrari up the road. The dog, barking, moved up the path to the house, a self-appointed herald. Before Cotter reached the house, two people came out on the front porch.

One of them was a young man with full brown beard, wearing blue jeans, boots, and a sheepskin-lined jacket over a blue workshirt. The other was a girl, blonde, with a red knitted scarf over her head and ears. Her figure wasn't visible under a heavy man's coat, much too large for her.

It was the girl who spoke. "Do something for you, Jack?"

"I'm looking for Scatback Hughes," Cotter said.

"He's not here," the girl said. Her young voice was hostile.

"When will he be back?"

"I don't have any idea," the girl said.

The collie dog sat down in front of Cotter, looking up at

131

him, tongue lolling, as if he were telling Cotter it was his move. Cotter bent down and stroked his head.

"My name is David Cotter," he said to the girl. "Unless I've been misinformed, Hughes will know who I am. For your benefit I'm not a cop, or an FBI agent, or any kind of law."

The young man with the beard smiled. "I got to admit I never saw a cop driving a car like that, man."

"I'm here because I need help, and Hughes and his people may be the only ones who can give it to me."

"Why should Scatback help you?" the girl asked.

"Maybe because he's a decent man," Cotter said. "Maybe because by helping me he could help himself. Please ask him if he'll talk to me."

"I told you he isn't here," the girl said.

The front door opened and a man stood there. He was black. He stood over six feet, taller than Cotter. He had the magnificent trim and muscled body of an athlete. Cotter thought he'd never seen such bright and penetrating black eyes. The man's vitality was almost shocking it was so evident, so strong.

"Let him come in, Patty," the black man said. He turned and walked back into the house. Watching him move was like watching a ballet dancer ready to spring into the air.

The girl and the bearded man stood to one side and Cotter went into the house.

He found himself in a large living room. The furniture was worn and old, but comfortable-looking. The whole place was meticulously clean and neat. A fire of huge logs burned on a wide stone hearth. The black man turned as the two others closed the door.

"We don't use last names here, David," he said. "I'm Scatback. This is Patty, and that's Carl. Take off your coat."

Cotter took off his coat and dropped it on a chair by the door. Scatback stood by the fire, his hands locked behind his back. Cotter thought he'd never seen anyone dominate a mo-

132

ment as Scatback did. He had seen Presidents and judges who riveted attention on themselves by the nature of their positions, but Scatback, totally unknown, made it on some kind of burning intensity.

The girl, having thrown off the oversized coat, revealed a lovely slim figure. She was wearing blue denim slacks and a wine-colored man's shirt, open at the neck. She sat down on the floor beside an old Morris chair. Scatback's chair, Cotter would have bet.

"You know who I am?" Cotter asked.

"You're Senator Farraday's man," Scatback said. His voice was low, almost musical. "You were here asking questions the day after Mac Crenshaw was shot. You went back to Washington the next day. You got back here in the middle of last night. While you were here the first time, you had conversations with Captain Shane, with Lester Owen, and with Jack Murphy, who's at death's door in the Brownsville Hospital at this moment. Yes, I know who you are, David."

"And do you know why I'm here now, Scatback?" Cotter smiled. "With that kind of spy system you must know."

"Somebody told you I know what happens wherever I am," Scatback said. He moved away from the fireplace and sat down in the Morris chair. Instantly the girl's blonde head rested against his thigh, and he stroked her golden hair with a slim, black hand. Patty Prentiss was her name, Cotter remembered. Moss had told him the Director had hoped to use her to turn Scatback to violence. That had been agent Austin's job, and Austin's throat had been cut and his body thrown in the Potomac River. Somehow the room seemed colder.

"But you don't know specifically why I'm here this morning?" Cotter asked.

"You hope I'll tell you things I have no intention of telling you," Scatback said.

"Your spy system has broken down," Cotter said.

133

Scatback's bright black eyes didn't flicker. "It's early in the day, man," he said. "We don't use such modern inventions as the telephone. Like everything man has invented to improve his state, the telephone has been diverted to destroy him. Would you believe a tap, man? Would you believe some eager beaver, shivering with cold, a headset at his ears, hoping against hope he'll hear me tell someone—on the phone, mind you—that I'm planning to bomb the White House? So we use what you might call smoke signals. Sometimes they're delayed, if the wind's in the wrong quarter. What have I missed, David?" His hand ruffled the girl's blonde hair as he talked, and then he smoothed it out again.

"You're in love," Cotter said.

"That's the name of the game, man. Perhaps not the way you mean, but love is the name of the game. And if your puritanical soul is revolted by the thought of this black skin mingling with that white skin, then the conversation had better be over."

"Don't be a damn fool," Cotter said. "I fell in love a little over thirty-six hours ago, and I *am* talking about man to woman. Suddenly it's all that matters in the whole world to me." His voice shook. "When your smoke signals come through, you will learn that this woman, who is suddenly everything, has been ripped off, abducted, could be manhandled or tortured to tell someone something she doesn't know she knows, could be dead because that something is too dangerous to someone."

Scatback's face was a black stone mask. "Your secretary, whose name is Julie, and who registered with you at the Gateway early this morning?" he asked.

"That is a fake," Cotter said. "I was trying to hide this girl's true identity. Her name is Margaret Branson, Maggie to her friends, and she was Mac Crenshaw's executive secretary. She doesn't know what she knows, but if she remembers, it will

134

reveal the reason for Mac Crenshaw's murder and the identity of the person who gave the order to have it done."

A log on the fire snapped and broke, and a cloud of sparks went up the chimney.

"I am helpless," Cotter said. "There is no one in this town I can trust. I will tell you that Jack Murphy was my eyes and ears here in Brownsville. He sent me a message to say that he was onto something. I got here too late to find out what it was. Why do I come to you? To begin with, Maggie was being followed in Washington. The man who followed her had the credentials of an FBI agent named Arthur Austin. Austin, whom I know had infiltrated your group here, Scatback, was murdered two weeks ago. You or your people could have done it. A man of mine was killed night before last when he set out to trace this man who was following Maggie. You could have done that, too. You could have sent a dedicated girl to kill Mac Crenshaw. If you did all those things, I'm wasting my time and there is no help for Maggie. I don't believe you did. I pray to God you didn't. Because I have no place to turn but to you."

Scatback looked down at the blond Patty Prentiss. His hand cupped her chin and lifted her face. There was adoration in her blue eyes. "If someone took you away from me, baby," Scatback said, "I might go to my worst enemy for help. I am not David's worst enemy. I'm not even his enemy, only the enemy of his way of life. Fix the man some coffee, baby, and we'll see if we can make some sense out of all this garbage."

Not all men's dreams are concerned with personal gain or personal power. Scatback Hughes, Cotter came to believe, was a man who wanted peace in its deepest and truest sense. He did not believe, as some men do, that the way to peace is by subduing dissent. He didn't believe that the way to fight evil is with evil. He didn't believe that the end justifies the means. He believed that we are a sick society, strangled by self-serving lies. He believed that the one way to present the truth to people was by demonstrating against the false. Going to jail on a trumped-up charge was a demonstration in itself. Submitting to attack by hard hats with clubs and stones was a demonstration in itself. Driving men to extremes revealed the sickness of their dreams.

It had been that way with Arthur Austin, the FBI agent who had joined Scatback's army. Early on Scatback had spotted him for what he was.

"And yet you let him stay on?" Cotter asked.

Scatback nodded. The girl had brought coffee. Carl, the young man with the beard, had put a fresh log on the fire. The winter world outside was as remote as the North Pole.

"The Director, the old Director, was a strange man," Scatback said. "He would have denied it, but he hated black men. How many black agents were there in the Bureau in his time? He hated me because I was black and making noises. He hated me until the bile rose right up into his eyes because of Patty." Scatback looked down and stroked the blonde head that was at his knee again. "When he was gone, the Bureau still played the same game with me. They were going to close the book on Scatback, and Arthur was their tool. Arthur knew we were here to demonstrate against certain candidates in the primaries. He would supply us with information that would lead us down a false alley. That alley would be booby-trapped. Something would happen to Patty, and I would react like a man and not an angel."

"And yet you let it develop?" Cotter asked.

"Because we knew what was coming. Because the trap wouldn't spring. Because we'd be able to reveal Austin and the Bureau for what they were—to the people of this country!"

"Did the plan involve the assassination of Crenshaw?"

"No," Scatback said, flat and positive.

"Then why was Austin killed? Were you responsible?"

"No."

"Who, then?"

"Some other case, maybe. I have a feeling Austin hated his job. Maybe he had threatened to quit."

"From my contacts I know he hated the job," Cotter said. "But he hadn't quit."

"Maybe he was planning to talk," Scatback said. "We live in a climate where secrets are revealed every day, like bees flying out of a hive. Men in high places go to bed at night sweating, afraid someone will tell the truth about them. A man with an untold secret isn't safe in this world. Like your girl Maggie."

Cotter felt his teeth clamp together.

Scatback looked at Cotter as though he was waiting for something.

"The girl who shot Mac Crenshaw?" Cotter asked.

Scatback's lips moved, revealing very white teeth in a smile. "No comment," he said.

"You know who she is?"

"No comment," Scatback said, "until I'm a little surer of

you, David. Suppose you aren't who you appear to be, and I tell you who the girl is—if I know—and I tell you who worked her up to a pitch to kill Crenshaw—if I know—and then you go to the law with what I tell you—?" Scatback shrugged.

"How can I persuade you that all I care about is finding Maggie? If you can help me—?"

"Time. We need a little time," Scatback said. "Oh, I know there is no time, but we can't go off, aimless, in all directions at once. But I will tell you one thing I'm certain of, David. The man who killed Arthur Austin is the man who hyped up that girl to kill Mac Crenshaw, is the man who killed your man Christie, is the man who tried to kill Jack Murphy, is the man who persuaded your Maggie to go off with him. A rose is a rose is a rose. Same man, same violence, same monstrous indifference to life and the pursuit of happiness."

"You're guessing!"

"Yes—and no. It has to be that way."

"Tell him, Scat," the blond girl said.

Scatback looked down at her, stroking her hair. "You trust him?"

"Yes I do."

"Woman's instinct?" Scatback smiled at her.

"The only reason I ever have for anything, Scat."

Scatback laughed. "Maybe that should be good enough for me," he said. The black eyes turned to Cotter. "People who join our group don't have to have a name," Scatback said. "That is to say, a real name. We don't ask if a name is real; we don't ask for a home address or a family pedigree. You believe like we do, welcome." Scatback's forehead was creased by a sudden frown. "We've got no special rules for living—except one. No hard drugs. Sex is communal. You can smoke a little pot if you want to. We happen to think it's less harmful than tobacco or liquor. I'm saying, people join us, we don't ask questions. We soon find out if they really believe the way we do, or if they've joined us because somebody told them this is a place for free sex, for orgies of some sort. That's the rumor spread by the law."

"What is it Patty wants you to tell me?" Cotter asked.

Scatback nodded. "Maybe a year, fourteen months ago, we were in the Middle West, picketing a big oil refinery just outside Cleveland. Two young people wandered in on us, a girl and a young man. They were what we call 'runaway types.' The girl from a good family somewhere. She was strung out on pot and sex. The boy, medium tall, brown beard and long brown hair, very bright. His name was Cal, he said. Her name was Marcia, she said. He talked our language, the language of dissent. He was so good at it I figured he must have been taught by smart people. But, somehow, he smelled bad to me. After about ten days it appeared to us that all he wanted was to screw all the girls, drink too much whiskey, torture Marcia by forcing her to sleep with other men when all she wanted was him. So I told them to move on. They weren't for us. And they moved. Did I tell you what the man's real name was?"

"Cal? No."

"He said it was Caligula."

"You're kidding!"

"Of course it wasn't his name," Scatback said. "He laughed when he told me. But around here we just don't ask. If it amused him to associate himself with a corrupt Roman emperor, that was his business. So Marcia and Cal moved on because we didn't want them around any more. I told you, more than a year ago."

"And a few days ago Marcia killed Mac Crenshaw?" Cotter asked.

Scatback nodded slowly. "I was dragged into the morgue by the State Police after the shooting. Was the dead girl one of us? I could answer truthfully that she wasn't. Did I know who she was? I could honestly say that I didn't. A year ago she had

139

called herself Marcia, but I didn't know then and I don't know now who she was. If I had admitted to the law that I had ever seen her, they'd have been all over us. Since I couldn't tell them who she was or where she came from—" Scatback shrugged.

"Had you seen her around here before the assassination?"

"No. That morning we pulled everybody back here to the farm. We didn't expect anything to happen, had no reason to think anything would. But just in case there was any kind of demonstration against Crenshaw, which could come from Lester Owen and his friends, we decided to stay here and be counted by Mildred and the two men who worked for her."

"Mildred?"

"Mrs. Dumphy, our landlady. Lucky we did, because the law couldn't hang anything on us. We think Marcia must have come into town that morning, after we'd pulled back. If she'd been there, say the day or the night before, some one of us would have seen her. We watch who comes into an area where we're located."

"And Cal—the man?"

"Not a sign of him since he left us in Cleveland more than a year ago," Scatback said. "He had Marcia ready to do anything in God's world he asked back then. Cal might be back of the Crenshaw killing, or that poor demented girl could have found a new Svengali by now."

"Can you describe Cal?"

"A type," Scatback said. "Long brown hair, a beard, blue jeans, leather jacket. When you've known them a while, you can tell them apart. Cal hasn't been in town since we got here —not before or after the shooting." The black man's eyes narrowed. "Of course, if he shaved off his beard, got himself a crew cut and a Brooks Brothers' suit, he might walk right by me on the street and I wouldn't know him. If I heard him speak, that would be something else again." He patted the blonde girl's hair, got up from his chair, and walked over to the fireplace. "We're not helping you, David. Talk isn't helping you. What could your girl Maggie know·that could make her so dangerous?"

And yet talk was all they had. In spite of the fire Cotter felt a cold chill settling in his bones. It was more than two hours now since Maggie had driven away from the Gateway Motel, apparently willingly, with the man in the brown parka. And in that time Cotter hadn't come even close to guessing why, or where to look, or who to challenge. He had never in his life felt so desperately helpless. Every minute that passed might be bringing Maggie closer to some unendurable crisis point, and he couldn't help.

"You can't chinashop it," Scatback said. "You can't bull around taking wild swings at everyone, David. It's a jigsaw puzzle and we have to try to fit the pieces together. If there's to be a chance for your woman, you have to be right on target when you move."

And so this strange, vibrant black man began to work at the puzzle, moving back and forth on the stone hearth, the fire behind him, like a college professor lecturing a class. The blonde girl, and the bearded young man, and Cotter were his class, his students.

"Whatever it is your Maggie knows, it has to do with Mac Crenshaw," Scatback said. "Whatever it is, it could expose what you have called the man behind the gun, David. She had been Mac's secretary and then his executive assistant. Anything personal between them?"

Cotter's voice sounded flat. "That kind of relationship always has a special closeness. If you're asking if she was his mistress, I can only say I don't think so."

"But she would know all his professional life, probably a good deal about his personal life. Right?"

"Right."

"Let's take what we know, which is damned little," Scatback said, pacing the hearth. "A girl I know as Marcia killed Mac. This girl had no convictions, no causes, no need for anything except to satisfy her neurotic hungers through sex and drugs. She could have been anyone's tool who helped her to those ends. The man I knew as Cal? Possibly, but in a year's time Marcia could have found someone else who directed her destiny. You must ask yourself was Marcia actually one of us, of my group. Are we behind all this? I know we aren't so I, working on the jigsaw, pass that by."

"I also pass," Cotter said.

"Thanks, friend," Scatback said, and smiled. "Mac was here in Brownsville on behalf of Senator Farraday. Is that why he was killed? Did he know something about Farraday's opposition that made someone want him dead?"

"He'd only been working for Farraday for about a month," Cotter said. "Wouldn't Farraday know what that was, if it exists? He doesn't. Would Maggie forget something that happened that recently?"

"Not likely," Scatback said. "There are people here in Brownsville who don't want Farraday to win the primary. Lester Owen for one. But Crenshaw's assassination will help Farraday, not hurt him. There is former Senator Cleary, who hated Mac's guts because Mac and the special prosecutor destroyed him. He might have blown a fuse. But use Marcia to do his dirty work? That would take time and careful preparation. It doesn't make sense to me. And it brings me to a question, David. The Cleary case is dead, gone, finished. The evidence is a matter of public record. Why would Cleary or Owen, his friend, be searching for evidence in Mac's office and Maggie's apartment?"

"No sensible reason," Cotter said.

"So for the moment let's eliminate Farraday's campaign as a reason for the assassination, and let's eliminate a Cleary

142

revenge as the motive. Searching for evidence suggests something connected to the Special Prosecutor's office."

"Mac quit the special prosecutor's office a month ago," Cotter said. "He turned over everything connected with that operation to Max Larkin, the prosecutor."

"The man behind the gun might not know that," Scatback said. "Or he might think something had come Mac's way since his resignation."

"But Maggie would know that," Cotter said. "Again, it's too recent for her to have forgotten. And wouldn't Larkin know? He says he doesn't."

"So, for the moment, we have to assume Mac wasn't killed for something connected with Farraday's campaign, and not because of something connected with the special prosecutor's business. Unlikely revenge by Cleary because of the complex use of Marcia. And let's go further, David. Marcia killed Mac. But there was a man following your Maggie in Washington; there was a man who killed your man Christie in Washington; there were people who searched an office and an apartment in Washington; there was a man who beat up Jack Murphy here in Brownsville; and there was a man, also in Brownsville, who persuaded your Maggie to go off with him. That sounds like a lot more than one man. It sounds like an organization, a group, a gang. It sounds like a group or gang on whom Mac had something, a group who arranged for Mac's death and searched for the evidence afterwards. And that rang no bell with your Maggie?"

"None."

"The answer's simple, David. You underrate your woman. She doesn't have a faulty memory. She doesn't remember because she doesn't know, wasn't told, knows of no incriminating documents. So she can't help the people who have taken her because she has no information."

"It seems odd Mac wouldn't tell her about anything so

143

important," the blonde girl said, speaking for the first time.

"Maybe not," Scatback said. "Maybe it was something very personal."

"Personal like what?" the girl asked.

"Like something about his wife, something about his father, something about his brother," Scatback said. His eyes were bright. His enormous energy seemed on the verge of taking off.

Cotter sat very still, his eyes fixed on Scatback. He could feel something beginning to cook inside him.

"By the sheerest coincidence," Scatback said, "Ross Crenshaw has an army, a private secret service. You could call them a group or a gang."

"That's too far-out, Scat," the girl said. "You're suggesting that Mac was murdered by his own father. That he used Marcia. That he— Oh, that's dream talk, Scat."

Cotter thought Scatback's eyes were burning holes in him. "I just thought of a funny," the black man said. "Marcus Aurelius Crenshaw. Marcus Aurelius, the good Roman emperor. And then there was Cal—Caligula, the bad Roman emperor. Brothers in the royal succession, you might say. What do you know about William Crenshaw, David?"

Cotter's pulse was pounding at his temples. "He left home a couple of years back. In trouble all over the country. Came home eight months ago, the prodigal son. Joined Mac when he went to work for Farraday."

"More than a year ago when Cal and Marcia joined us in Cleveland, one of us in those days was a traitor. His name was Arthur Austin. He was an FBI agent, as you know. He knew Cal in that stretch of time. Knew him, at least, as a runaway who joined our group with Marcia. Maybe, two weeks ago, he saw Cal again and this time knew who he was and where he came from. It might have been dangerous to Cal for Austin to know that."

"Dream talk!" the blonde girl protested. "You're saying that

144

Cal is Bill Crenshaw, that he programmed Marcia to kill his brother. That's crazy, Scat. Bill Crenshaw killed Marcia trying to save his brother."

"Or to keep her from talking after she'd done what he set her up to do," Scatback said in a level, quiet voice.

Cotter stood up. The jigsaw was coming together, incredible but coming together. The blonde girl was still protesting. Did Scatback really think Bill Crenshaw was using his father's army, his goons, his secret service, to murder the Old Man's own son, the dream-son who was to be President of the United States, and then to cover up the crime? Cotter remembered something Maggie had said. "Ross Crenshaw is a terrifying creature."

"Ross Crenshaw would murder his own mother if it would buy him an extra barrel of oil," Scatback said. "It would be interesting to know what Jack Murphy smelled out."

"You're just dreaming something up!" The blonde girl was making a last try.

"There is a way to settle it," Scatback said. "Let me get a close look at Bill Crenshaw and hear him talk. I'll know then if he is Caligula."

Outside the farmhouse the skies had clouded over and a cold wind rattled the glass in the windows. It was, as the blonde girl had said, a crazy pattern that Scatback had woven for them, and yet, somehow, it was irresistible. It was, of course, totally without proof at the moment, but it pointed a way to go. It would be a fascinating trail for an investigator to follow. But not Cotter. If he believed for a moment that Bill Crenshaw and Ross Crenshaw were behind the murder of Mac Crenshaw, the murders of Arthur Austin, of Red Christie, and the brutal attack on Jack Murphy, then he had to believe that someone in the Crenshaw complex was responsible for Maggie's disappearance.

"You don't need me to tell you," Scatback said in that hard yet bright voice of his, "that it appears your woman left the Gateway Motel with someone she knew and was prepared to believe. The motel woman told you she 'walked around to the other side of the car and got in.' Would she have gone away with a Crenshaw?"

Cotter tried to remember exactly what he and Maggie had said about Mac's people after he'd taken her away from the Virginia house over the Old Man's angry demand that she stay. They hadn't dreamed the Crenshaws were involved in anything but the desire to catch Mac's killer, the man behind the gun, and destroy him. He'd warned Maggie they'd use her without regard for the danger in which it might place her. That they themselves might be the killers, intent on covering their crimes, had never occurred to Cotter or to Maggie.

"She might," Cotter said, in a voice he didn't recognize as his own. "If they told her that I was in trouble, or that I'd asked them to bring her to me. They were Mac's family, Mac's people. She couldn't have dreamed that they—I'm not sure that I can believe that they—"

"Believe," Scatback said, "and face the hard facts, David. It's still a guess, still a theory, but it's the only explanation that fits. Mac Crenshaw was a decent man. His father is a ruthless pirate. Bill—if he is the Cal I know—is a selfish, self-serving little monster. The Old Man's world empire is built on the unprincipled destruction of his competition, his business rivals. Suppose he had involved himself in some plan to plow under opposition somewhere. It could be aimed at a rival corporation, or at a government somewhere in the Third World, the under-developed world of oil. It could be something damaging to his own country or some ally of the American government. Try Israel on for size. A big, wicked conspiracy that would leave innocent people dead and dying. That kind of scheme is not unusual for Ross Crenshaw. Mac is the crown prince, his heir.

But Mac is decent. Suppose he was told or stumbled on this scheme of his father's. He gathers the facts, the evidence that will prove his father's complicity after the deed is done. Then he goes to his father and says no dice, stop here. He has him by the short hairs. Now Ross Crenshaw won't take that kind of order from anyone; not from the Golden Boy, the future President. He needs help, but who can he go to? Not to his paid mercenaries. He can't go to a hit man and say, 'I have to get rid of my son.' He would be blackmailed out of his shorts after that. But there is someone, someone who hates Mac, has been jealous of him all his life, hates him for his success, his glamorous popularity. Bill, the crazy son, the gone son, the debauched son. Caligula, Cain, call him what you like. The Old Man brings Bill home, takes him up onto the mountain and shows him the world. It can all be his if Bill will undertake the pleasant chore of eliminating Mac."

"God Almighty!" Cotter whispered.

"Bill has a weapon no one would ever dream of connecting with the Crenshaws—the depraved, sex-crazy, drug-sodden Marcia. Ross Crenshaw has time, months if necessary. Mac has to go and the evidence of the conspiracy be retrieved. But there can't be a breath of suspicion attached to it."

"Crenshaw persuaded Mac to give up his job with the special prosecutor and hit the trail for Farraday," Cotter said, remembering. "It was supposed to prepare him for his own shot at the Presidency eight years from now."

"It was supposed to set him up for an assassin's bullet," Scatback said. "It is so well staged, so well planned, that no one on earth would guess the truth, not even your Maggie. Mac is shot. Bill is a near hero trying to save him. Of course he is just making sure Marcia never talks. Then they go after the evidence and can't find it. A terrible fear overtakes them. Maybe Mac shared what he knew with someone else, even though he may have assured them he wouldn't. Maybe he passed the evidence on to someone for safekeeping, warning them how explosive it was. The first person they think of is Mac's trusted secretary, his executive assistant, maybe a woman who loves him. Because maybe she did, David."

"Maybe," Cotter said.

"They hope to find out if she knows. They have her followed. Then you get into the act. Could she have told you? They must have known that you spent a night with her. Your man Christie was killed by someone who was watching her, someone Christie recognized. Could it have been Bill Crenshaw?"

"George Zachery, who is head of Crenshaw's security force, was in town," Cotter said. "Christie was thrown off the Washington police force for being too tough on Zachery."

"It doesn't matter much who any more, except to the police who will have to wrap this up," Scatback said. "All that matters to us, to you, David, is that Ross Crenshaw is the power behind it all. To proceed, they don't find the evidence they're looking for in Mac's office or in Maggie's apartment. You can be sure they've been through that Virginia house from roof to cellar. They have to try the only thing left to them. Maggie was dead loyal to Mac. Maybe she hasn't told you anything. Maybe she is following instructions from Mac—in case anything happened to him. They can't risk it. They have to get her away somewhere, persuade her to talk if she knows anything." Scatback's face was carved out of black marble. "And they can never let her go, David, now that she knows about them."

A spasm of rage shook Cotter's whole body. He had to go somewhere. He had to find her. Yet there was no place to go. He could kill them, he could murder them, he could cut them to pieces, but that wouldn't get her back.

"As long as they think she may know where the evidence is, they will keep her alive," Scatback said, "though God knows what they will do to her to get her to talk. We can only hope to find her before it's too late."

"You say 'we,' Scat," the blonde girl said. "It's not our problem! It's not our ball game!"

"We have been fighting the Crenshaws of this world since the beginning, Patty," Scatback said gently. "We can't quit when there is a real fight to fight."

3

What Cotter might have done without the cooling influence of Scatback, he would never know. His impulse was to say, "Let's go! Let's get out of here! Let's get it done!" But get what done? Find the Crenshaws, the Old Man and Bill, and take them apart, physically, violently? Even if that was possible with the Old Man surrounded by his army, his security people, his guards, what would that do for Maggie? The Crenshaws would face death rather than admit publicly to the murder of a son and brother, because that admission would be the same as dying; the end of an empire, the end of power, the end of everything that mattered to them. And it would take time—time, a commodity they couldn't afford. How long could Maggie hold out? How would they try to force her to tell something she didn't know? Once they were convinced she didn't know what they wanted to find out, they couldn't let her go. They could never let her go, and she would only live as long as they still thought she knew a secret.

Time!

Go to Washington and confront the Crenshaws? Even if he had wings, it would take a day, God knows how much longer. They would stall, and fight, and claw, and the minute they suspected that he knew the truth, a signal would go out, somehow, and Maggie would have had it.

"You can't chinashop it," Scatback had said.

He said other things now in that cool, analytic voice. "You can't go after a man-eating tiger with a water pistol, David," he said. "I know what torture delay must be to you, but we have to act sensibly and with a purpose. If it takes too long, then God help us all. But to be scatterbrained about it is to have no chance at all."

He was right, of course. Cotter, the palms of his hands damp with sweat, waited for something practical to be suggested.

"Maggie may be close by," Scatback said, "or she may be hundreds of miles away from here by now. One thing we can be certain of. The Crenshaws have this town covered like a tent. In ordinary times strangers stand out like sore thumbs in Brownsville. But this isn't an ordinary time. There are politicians campaigning for the primary; there are weekend skiers; there are hordes of reporters and special cops interested in the assassination. Among them are Crenshaw people, hidden by the simple influx of scores of strangers. Who knows who is who? Which means that you are being watched, David, but you don't know who to watch or who is watching you. Make any kind of move that's dangerous to them and they'll try to stop you."

"If I only knew something that would be dangerous to them," Cotter said.

"The truth!" Scatback said. "Let me see Bill Crenshaw and hear him talk and I'll know if he's Cal. Find out what smelled like Limburger cheese to Jack Murphy. But we have to go our separate ways."

"Separate?"

"Be openly connected with us and there'll be hell to pay," Scatback said. His voice had turned bitter. "It won't take much in this town to start a lynch-mob action against us. Crenshaw's people could start it; Lester Owen and his friends would support it. We'd all be useless, helpless, fighting for ourselves instead of looking for Maggie."

The beginnings of a plan emerged. Cotter was to leave the farm at once, his aim to get to a phone and contact Julie Hartman in his Washington office. His people there might be

151

able to find out where the Old Man and Bill Crenshaw were at the moment. While he waited for a report, he would try to pick up Jack Murphy's trail, who the old reporter had talked to, where he had been the last day or two. From all accounts he had lived in the bar at Hunter's Lodge. What he had seen or heard must have been there.

Meanwhile Scatback's army would begin circulating in Brownsville, ostensibly to demonstrate against conservative candidates in the primary, actually to try to pick out Crenshaw people in town. Once they had spotted one or two of them, they might lead to something.

"We'll be watching the watchers if we can pick them out," Scatback said.

Communication between Cotter and Scatback's army would be difficult. The farmhouse phone was tapped. Mrs. Dumphy's phone was tapped.

"Someone will jog your elbow somewhere," Scatback said, "and you'll know he—or she—is from us. We'll be looking for you in the neighborhood of Hunter's Lodge."

And so down the mountain went the red Ferrari toward the Grandma Moses town in the valley. The first time Cotter had seen it from that perspective it had looked charming and peaceful to him. Now, somehow, it seemed to him to be crawling with evil. As he parked the Ferrari across the street from Hunter's Lodge, faces, red from the wind-blown cold, seemed hostile, suspicious. Natives wondered who strangers were and strangers wondered who strangers were.

It was midafternoon and the bar and grill at Hunter's Lodge was busy. Out-of-town press people seemed to have taken it over as a kind of headquarters. Any new face that appeared was a possible story or the source for a story. The local man, Riley, wasn't among them. Cotter supplied himself with a pocketful of change from a bartender who eyed him curiously. He went to the pay phone booth which was located in a little alcove off the main grill room. He tried something absurd at first. He called the Gateway Motel and found himself connected with the gaudy Mrs. Ramsey. Had there been any message from "Mrs. Hartman"? Or had she returned to Cabin J? Of course the answer was no to both questions. He wondered what else he'd expected. That Maggie was there, safe and sound, and would explain that she'd gone off with an old college chum for a cup of coffee? Maggie was in the hands of killers.

Then Cotter, angry at himself for indulging in childish hopes, put in a collect call to the real Mrs. Hartman in Washington. He sketched the situation as briefly as he could, and Julie sounded shaken.

"What can we do, David?" she asked.

"I want to be able to put my hands on both the Crenshaws, Ross and Bill," he said. "I want to know if they're in Washington, or at the Virginia house, or where they've gone if they're not there."

"No one connected with them is going to tell us anything," Julie said. "It might take hours to get a lead."

"Try Gwen Crenshaw, Mac's wife," Cotter said. "Tell her I'm anxious to get in touch with Bill or her father-in-law. That I've turned up something important in Brownsville."

"You want them to know where you are, David?"

"They know," Cotter said bitterly. "The woods are alive with Crenshaw people."

"How do I reach you?" Julie asked.

"No way. I'll call you. Get on it, Julie."

He went back to the bar. What did he do, stand here and have a drink while somewhere Maggie was being tortured to tell something she didn't know—if they hadn't already wiped her out?

Warren Hunter, the proprietor of the lodge, had taken the place of the bartender who'd supplied Cotter with change. He had shrewd dark eyes that seemed to be constantly studying

153

every face in the grill room, on the lookout for trouble that didn't seem to be brewing.

"I wondered when you'd be dropping by again, Mr. Cotter," he said in a voice that was scarcely above a whisper. He was apparently busy polishing a bar glass.

"You know who I am?" Cotter said.

"Knowing who people are is my business," Hunter said, rubbing at the glass. His mouth moved stiffly, like a man who was afraid there were lip readers around. "Murph is my friend —and yours."

"How do you know that?"

"He used my office phone to try to reach you in Washington. I heard the message he left for you, about smelling Limburger cheese."

Cotter rested his hands on the bar to keep them from shaking. "Did he tell you what it was that smelled?"

"He told me you were Farraday's man, looking for whoever it was who triggered that girl. I think he thought he had something."

"What?"

"Martin Cleary," Hunter said.

"The former Senator? Too obvious, Mr. Hunter. The whole world knew he had it in for Mac Crenshaw. He'd be the first person the FBI would grab if there was the slightest evidence." Cotter felt disappointment. If that was what Jack Murphy had, it wasn't promising.

"Murph was pretty tight when he called you," Hunter said. "But he made an effort to sober up because he thought you'd be coming. He talked to me because he trusted me. I'd give a good deal to see the people who beat him up caught and crucified. He talked about Cleary to me, but not as though he thought he might be the one who planned to kill Mac Crenshaw. 'Martin-baby has friends you wouldn't dream he'd have,' he said. 'Did you ever figure out how Martin-baby got so rich

154

just when everything went sour for him? He wasn't any use to anyone out of the Senate, but that's when he got rich.' "

"Got rich?" Cotter said.

"Mac Crenshaw exposed him as a bribe-taking crook," Hunter said. "Got him impeached. But right after that he bought the old Powers estate. Must have cost him a hundred and fifty thousand. More thousands fixing it up. He's got servants out there. He was a small-town lawyer with no money to speak of before that. Suddenly he's spending like a millionaire."

"The local gossip?" Cotter asked.

"Someone was paying him for something," Hunter said. "He settled in town, didn't go anywhere, wasn't doing anything for anyone here, but the money was rolling in from somewhere. Murphy said if I knew who Cleary's friends were, there'd be no mystery about it."

"But he didn't tell you who they were?"

Hunter shook his head. "I tried to tease him out of it, but he just grinned at me and said he was saving it for you. You were entitled to it first, he said. I tell you, because it might help you to find out who beat up on him."

"Local friends, out-of-town friends?" Cotter asked.

"His local friend is Lester Owen. You know him. You were in here with him earlier. Owen and some of his cronies go out to play poker with Cleary a couple of nights a week. Murphy couldn't have meant them, because everyone knows that. There was nothing surprising about that. I thought he was talking about some out-of-town big shot."

"Someone out of his Washington past?"

"That's the way I figured it," Hunter said. "All the money in the world is in Washington, or controlled by Washington, by the lobbies, by the corporations that own the world. That bad smell Murph mentioned? I figured it was blackmail of some sort. That kind of thing would be right up Martin Cleary's

155

alley." Then Hunter seemed to stiffen behind the bar. "Sorry," he said. "We're about to get snowed under. Young Crenshaw promised the press and the media an interview."

The name spun Cotter around where he stood. Moving from the front entrance toward the gathered reporters was a shyly smiling Bill Crenshaw. The fleece-lined overcoat and ski cap were Abercrombie & Fitch, the tweed sports jacket and gray flannel slacks were Brooks Brothers. The pale eyes behind the wire-rimmed glasses were diffident, offering friendship to the reporters who crowded around him.

An anger, a rage more intense than any emotion Cotter could remember swept over him. That smiling sonofabitch knew where Maggie was and what had happened to her or was happening to her. He wanted to get his hands on Bill Crenshaw, tear the truth out of his throat. He actually took a step forward when a hand closed on his arm. Cotter looked down, prepared to shake off restraint violently. A young man with a vague face and a waiter's apron tied round him was the restrainer.

"Keep your cool, David," the young man said. "Scat can't come in here. His face is too black. When Crenshaw leaves here, try to stall him outside the front entrance, talk to him about anything. Scat will be listening and then we'll know for sure."

The young man went out into the room, picking up soiled glasses from various tables. "Someone will jog your elbow," Scat had promised.

Cotter turned his back on the scene and faced the back bar, his hands gripping the edge of the mahogany, his knuckles white. He could hear the gist of the press conference. The questions were jumbled but the answers from Bill Crenshaw were clear.

He had two reasons for being back in Brownsville, Bill Crenshaw told the reporters. The police had many questions to ask him that he'd been too shaken up to answer earlier—questions that might establish some kind of motive for his brother's murder. And second, he was taking over his brother's job as the manager of the primary campaign for Senator Farraday. Plans made by Mac some time ago would have to be changed.

"My brother was a national figure," Bill said. "His appearance could help the Senator." The shy smile was quite charming. "I'm just a tour guide, a travel agent. No one would turn out to see me, or listen to me . . . Yes, I think the Senator will make more appearances than he'd planned."

A reporter attracted enough silence to ask: "Has anything developed that makes you think there was any kind of conspiracy involved in your brother's assassination, Mr. Crenshaw? Something more than the act of a drug-crazed girl?"

"The police, the FBI, and CrenAm's own security people are, to coin a cliché, leaving no stone unturned," Bill said, smiling. "Seriously, there's always that possibility, and we'll keep working at it until we're satisfied that it was no more than the irresponsible act of a psychotic juvenile."

Cotter edged his way along the bar and down the far wall to the front entrance. He didn't know if Bill saw him. If their eyes met, he would have to stop and speak, and their conversation must take place outside where Scatback could overhear it. Cotter's pulse pounded at his temples and wrists. It took every ounce of control he had to keep from charging across the room and smashing Bill Crenshaw's shy, smiling face. The bastard!

Brownsville moved at its own relaxed pace. Scatback was nowhere to be seen, but across the way he spotted the blonde Patty looking in the window of a small boutique. The cold wind struck at Cotter as though he was an enemy. He leaned against the wall of the lodge porch, waiting for Bill to come out.

Cotter felt a faint gleam of hope. Bill Crenshaw's presence here could mean that Maggie wasn't too far away. If they were still trying to pry something out of her, Bill wouldn't want to

157

be too far away if she finally told them something or if she had to be eliminated. Cotter thought the decision would have to be Bill's, or at least Bill's as the agent for his father. Or perhaps there was no decision to make. What must happen to Maggie was predetermined, no matter whether she helped or not. Cotter asked himself whether Maggie would have gone away from the Gateway Motel with Bill. It was possible if Bill told her he had a message from Cotter to meet somewhere. In spite of warnings Maggie probably still thought of the Crenshaws as civilized people, ruthless but civilized. She had walked right into it.

Drawn up just south of the lodge was a black limousine with a driver sitting behind the wheel. The afternoon sun struck the windshield in such a way that Cotter couldn't see the driver's face. Somehow it looked like a Crenshaw automobile, a Cadillac. Cotter strained to catch sight of Scatback somewhere. No sign of him.

And then, almost unexpectedly, Bill Crenshaw walked out the front door of the lodge and came face to face with Cotter. He didn't seem surprised.

"I thought I saw you at the bar, David," he said, "but I wasn't sure when you didn't join the party."

Cotter fought to make his voice sound casual. "I didn't want to get involved in the press conference," he said, "but I did want to speak to you."

Bill Crenshaw frowned. It was a sympathetic frown. "Captain Shane told me that your secretary had disappeared and that you are concerned."

Why pretend? Cotter thought. They knew. "It isn't my secretary," he said. "It's Maggie Branson. I was trying to keep her under cover because I feel she's in danger."

Bill nodded. "Man following her, the search of her office and apartment. She didn't leave you a message?"

"Just went off, apparently willingly, with an unidentified

158

man. She must have been persuaded that he had a message from me."

"What have you done?"

"Notified the police, what else?" Cotter said.

"God, this is a nasty mess," Bill said. "I let the reporters in there think we didn't seriously consider there was anyone involved but that deranged girl. But we have to believe there is someone else, don't we?"

Yes, you sonofabitch, we do, Cotter thought. He just answered, "Yes." Take him by the throat, right here on the main street, and choke it out of him! First they must know for sure, yet Scatback was nowhere. The blonde girl was still studying the boutique window across the way.

"I'll be around for another day, trying to get things reorganized here," Bill said. "If there's anything we can do to help? Some of Father's people are here in town."

"So I imagined," Cotter said.

"Because of course we don't believe it was just the girl," Bill said. "I'm staying at the Brownsville Ski Club up the mountain. If you want to get in touch—or we can help." He hesitated. "Do you have any idea what it is someone thinks Maggie knows?"

Cotter's teeth made a grinding sound, they were clamped so hard together. They think she may know why you murdered your brother, you bastard! "No idea," he said. "Nor does she."

Bill shook his head. "It's a crazy world we're living in," he said. "Bribery and corruption in business, the Lockheed scandal, for example; bribery and corruption in politics, Watergate, for example; kidnaping and murder, a part of everyday life."

And you and your old man are masters of all those arts, Cotter thought. He said: "And too many people think it's just business as usual, politics as usual, murder as usual. That's what our man Farraday is fighting."

Bill's smile took on a faintly cynical twist. "That's what they all say they're fighting," he said. The smile faded. "Mac would have been the exception if he'd lived to get to it. An honest politician."

And that was something you couldn't risk, Cotter thought. He was shaking, not with cold but with frustration and anger. His moment with Bill Crenshaw was going to come, he told himself. But not now, not yet.

"Again, if there's anything we can do to help," Bill said. "Naturally, we're concerned about Maggie. She was indispensable to Mac. We all owe her. Let us know if you get any news, and, of course, we'll contact you if we pick up anything. Where can I reach you?"

"I'm registered at the Gateway," Cotter said. As you damn well know! "But Warren Hunter here at the lodge will take a message for me."

Bill started down the three steps to the sidewalk, and then turned back. "Captain Shane tells me that this fellow Murphy who was beaten up was a friend of yours, working for you."

"Just as a friend, he was keeping an eye open for me."

"Had he reported anything interesting to you?"

Cotter still fought to keep his voice level. "A bad smell," he said. "But not what it was."

Bill hunched his shoulders into his fleece-lined coat. "This doesn't seem to be a very healthy town for decent people," he said, and headed for the Cadillac.

Across the way the blonde girl had turned from the boutique window and was watching. The big car turned in such a sharp U that Cotter never got a look at the driver, except that he was a big man. For a moment Cotter thought he was letting them get away. The Ferrari was only a few yards further down the street. He could run the Cadillac into the ground if he had to. But the blonde girl was coming briskly toward him now. She slowed down as she came close to Cotter and then walked slowly past him as though she didn't see him.

160

"He is Cal," she said.

"Where's Scatback?"

"About ten yards behind you in the alley between buildings. He gave me the sign. Don't worry, one of our people is tailing them."

Even as she spoke, Cotter saw a young man with a crash helmet hiding his head and face take off on a small Japanese motorcycle.

The blonde girl was gone, walking briskly once more. Cotter turned back toward the lodge and the alley that separated it from a small mom-and-pop grocery store. Standing about ten feet deep in the alley was the tall figure of Scatback Hughes, swathed in a long overcoat that he must have found in a thrift shop somewhere. A knitted blue toque was pulled down over his ears. His white teeth glittered in his black face in what was a grimace, not a smile.

"Cold!" he muttered. "That's one of the reasons I quit football. We had to play games in Minnesota in December!" He blew on his hands. "It's the damnedest thing, David. I could have been as close to that sonofabitch as I am to you and I wouldn't have known him! Those clothes! That Madison Avenue haircut. Those schoolteacher glasses! He never wore glasses when he was with us. But that soft way of talking I'd know anywhere. He'd talk soft like that just as he was about to slip a shiv between your ribs. You recognize the driver of his car?"

Cotter shook his head. "The sun was reflected on the windshield. I couldn't get a look."

Scatback's voice was harsh. "George Zachery, the Old Man's expert in violence. He's the expert at making people talk. Expert at burning you with cigarette butts, expert at driving wooden wedges under your fingernails, expert at using sex as an assault weapon, expert at cutting you to pieces one ball at a time!"

161

"Stop it!" Cotter almost shouted. That monster had worked on Maggie, might still be working on Maggie.

Scatback's black eyes were so cold they looked frozen in their sockets. "One of my people fell into his hands a year or so ago," he said. "A brave boy of nineteen. He was delivered to us, or what was left of him, which provided me with all the proof I need to tell you what I tell you."

Cotter thought of Maggie and thought he was going to be sick there in the alley.

"You're carrying a gun," Scatback said.

Cotter had taken his Police Special out of the luggage in the Ferrari when he'd left Stemkowski's house to head for Scatback's farm. Instinctively his hand reached for where it was tucked into his belt.

"Don't use it till you know for sure," Scatback said.

"Know what for sure?"

"That your woman is dead," Scatback said in a flat, cold voice. "Use a gun in Zachery's world and you may get him, but you won't walk five feet away without an army opening up on you. After you know she's dead, you may not care. Before that, David, she needs you cold, and clever, and in total control. Like I said before, don't chinashop it."

Cotter breathed air deep into his lungs. "But where do I start, Scatback?"

"He told you where he's staying, the Brownsville Ski Club. But that isn't where they've got your woman, a place crowded with weekend vacationers. They want her somewhere no one can hear her screams."

"God damn you!" Cotter said.

"So you have to face reality, David. If the job on your woman isn't finished, you can count on it that Zachery and the new crown prince of CrenAm will be in at the kill. Unless we're very unlucky, we'll know every place they go from now on."

"One boy on a motorcycle?"

162

"And a dozen others following him," Scatback said. "This is a game we've learned how to play expertly, David, and we'll play it for you up to the hilt. We know Bill Crenshaw and Zachery are here. Did you have any luck locating the Old Man?"

"My people in Washington are working on it. I have to call back."

"So call. In the long run the Old Man may be your only chance, David. He's the only person who can stop those sadistic bastards."

"Why would he stop them?"

"He stopped his own favorite son, didn't he? In Ross Crenshaw's world of violent power people are just pawns, no matter how close they are to him. If we could get the slightest clue as to what Mac Crenshaw had on his father; if we knew what your friend Murphy had seen or heard—"

Cotter stood very still. It was almost as if the combination to a safe was falling into place in his head. His lips moved stiffly as he told Scatback what Warren Hunter had told him, about the strange friends that Martin Cleary, the former Senator, had, and his sudden wealth.

"It's not much, man, but by God it's something," Scatback said.

Back inside the Lodge, Cotter called Washington again. Julie Hartman was ready for him.

"Not too much luck, David," she said. "But I did get to talk to Gwen Crenshaw. She thinks Bill may be in Brownsville."

"He is. I've just seen him."

"She has no idea where the Old Man is, or how to find out. It's a case of 'Don't call us, we'll call you.' But she says she wants to talk to you, David. She says it's urgent. She gave me her own private number. You're to call at the first opportunity. That was an hour ago."

163

Cotter called the private number. There was no answer. He called the number of the main house. The estate manager, Bishop, answered the phone. Mrs. Crenshaw had gone into Washington. He had no idea where, or when she could be expected back. Cotter persisted.

"Look, Mr. Cotter, Crenshaws don't tell the slaves what their plans are. 'Have my car brought around, Bishop.' That's all I know."

"And you don't have any idea where I can reach the Old Man?"

"Only Bill and George Zachery could tell you that, and I don't have a notion where they are."

Cotter didn't enlighten him. He left the phone booth and walked over to the bar where Warren Hunter was still working behind the stick.

"Where is Cleary's house—the old Powers place?" he asked.

"About three miles out of town on Route Twelve," Hunter said. "You'll pass a big dairy farm about three miles out of town. It has BYWOOD DAIRY painted on the barn roof. Maybe a quarter of a mile past that, on the left, you'll see some big stone gates. That's the Powers place." He shook his head. "Takes a while for things to change around here, Mr. Cotter. People still call it 'the Powers place' even though Martin Cleary owns it."

The sun, low in the west, painted the mountaintops a startling scarlet. The early winter night would be closing in before another hour passed, and Cotter wanted to get a look at Cleary's place in the daylight. It could be he'd want to be able to find his way around there after darkness had closed in. If Scatback's people detected Bill Crenshaw or Zachery headed for Cleary's, that might explain Jack Murphy's mutterings about 'strange friends.' As far as the public knew, the Crenshaws were Martin Cleary's mortal enemies. Mac had disgraced him, driven him from office.

164

Route 12 was a narrow, two-lane highway. Signs indicated it led to someplace called Riverton. When he approached the Bywood Dairy, Cotter saw that the barn windows at ground level were all brightly lighted. Milking time, Cotter guessed. There was no one in sight to be interested in the red Ferrari.

The stone gates of the Powers place loomed up exactly as Hunter had promised. What he had not told Cotter was that there'd be a heavy metal chain blocking the driveway between the gates. Beyond the gates the driveway, carefully plowed, led through a thick stretch of woods. The house must lie beyond those woods, invisible from the main road.

Cotter got out of his car and went over to examine the chain. It was locked at both ends by heavy padlocks. Out of nowhere came a voice, hollow-sounding. Cotter thought it must be coming through some kind of speaker system. He looked up and around but couldn't spot anything.

"Unless you're expected, Senator Cleary isn't receiving guests," the voice said. "And I happen to know you're not expected."

"How do I get in touch with Mr. Cleary?" Cotter asked.

"Unless you've got his private phone number, you write him a letter," the voice said.

"It's important," Cotter said, stalling, trying to locate the speaker through which the voice came.

"If it was important, the Senator would have left word about it," the voice said. "You'd better move on, mister."

Instinct told Cotter that along with this metallic voice was a gun. The retired Senator was protecting himself rather extraordinarily for this rural countryside. If you guarded so carefully against intrusion by strangers, it could mean you had something to hide. Cotter felt a tingling sensation along his spine. This could be where they had Maggie, a place, as Scatback had suggested, where no one could hear her scream. His impulse was to get back in the car and jam the Ferrari through

165

the chain.

"Don't chinashop it," Scatback had warned.

The cold was bitter, and he was grateful for the warmth of the car as he got in behind the wheel again. He turned and headed slowly back in the direction of the dairy farm. It was still light enough to study the roadside. The woods came right down to the edge of the road, and as far as Cotter could see there was no fence, no obstacle of any kind to prevent his parking the car and walking through the woods to get a view of the house. It was worth a try, he thought.

He pulled as far over to the side of the road as he could, turned on his parking lights, got out of the car and headed into the woods. The going was rough. Nothing had been done to thin out years of growth. The brush was high and stubborn. The snow was waist-deep. Cotter found he had to literally wedge his way forward every step. By the time he came out into a clearing, night was total. But the house was there, lit up like a holiday festival. There were lights in windows on three levels. There were spotlights in trees outside the house that illuminated a pillared front entrance and the whole approach. It looked like a place expecting guests—or intruders. There'd be no way to get within fifty yards of the house without being clearly visible to anyone watching. Someone would be watching, Cotter knew. This was a fortress, not the gracious residence of a retired public servant.

Cotter stared at the blazing windows. Maggie might be behind one of them, he told himself, still holding out, please God, in some fashion. There was no way to attack the place alone. It would only provide them with another hostage, another victim. But an attack couldn't wait. He had to find Scatback and his army, the only people who could be trusted.

Cotter began to run back along the trail he'd made coming in. He was choking for breath before he'd gone too far, his face cut by a bramble thorn. They were out of time, he told himself.

166

He had just reached the edge of the woods when he saw that a light was focused on the red Ferrari. He crouched for a moment, trying to see. The high wind might have blotted out the sound of his coming. A man was walking slowly around the Ferrari, clear in the beam of a single bright light behind it. It all came into focus for Cotter then. A motorcycle, and the curious man was wearing a blue crash helmet.

Cotter stepped out into the clear, and instantly the man ducked down behind the far side of the Ferrari.

"David?" a tense voice asked.

Cotter let out his breath in a long sigh. Scatback's people never used last names. This was the young man on the Japanese bike. Cotter moved forward into the light of the bike's single lamp. The young man straightened up and took off his crash helmet. He was the bearded young man named Carl who had been in on the whole story at Scatback's farm.

"I saw your car," Carl said. "I was worried something had happened to you."

"You were looking for me?" Cotter asked.

"No. You knew I was following Crenshaw and Zachery?" He used last names for his enemies, Cotter thought. "Zachery drove Crenshaw to the Brownsville Ski Club. They had a drink at the bar and then split. I didn't have any instructions from Scat except to follow them and report. I thought I'd better stick to the one who was on the move. Zachery drove to some stone gates just up the road."

"There's a chain blocking the way," Cotter said.

"Right, but Zachery had a key to unfasten the chain. He drove in, put the chain back in place, and drove off through the woods."

"You know what's up that driveway?"

Carl nodded. "Cleary, that Senator Mac Crenshaw put out of business. Strange a Crenshaw man would have a key to his kingdom."

167

That was what Jack Murphy had thought. Zachery at the house meant fresh horrors for Maggie, if she was still alive.

"Where do we find Scatback?" Cotter asked.

"I'll find him," Carl said. "You wait at Hunter's Lodge. Someone will contact you."

Cotter brought his fist down on the fender of the Ferrari. "There's a chance Maggie is in there," he said. "The people responsible for what's happened to her are in there. I'm waiting here in case someone decides to take off. Tell Scatback I can't wait much longer, chinashop or no chinashop."

4

The motorbike made a roaring sound as Carl started it and then disappeared down the road toward the dairy farm. Cotter got into the Ferrari and started the motor. The cold outside the car was bone-biting. The motor would get a little heat circulating. He planned to turn the car and head back up the road until he had the stone gates in his sights. If Zachery or anyone else came out, they could turn either way on Route 12. Then Cotter thought of that metallic voice that had barred his way in. Someone was located somewhere who could see the gates. He had better not park in view or these people, as they had from the beginning, would be one jump ahead of him.

Cotter turned off his engine and sat huddled behind the wheel, listening. He had to be able to hear if someone drove out through those gates above him. The cold began to crowd in on him, and a frosty coating of ice to form on his windshield and windows. He needed his motor to activate his defroster, but he also needed to hear. The Ferrari's double exhaust system made it anything but quiet.

He sat there in pitch darkness, dreaming of vengeance, tortured by doubts.

Scatback had invented the Crenshaw involvement out of whole cloth, and yet there were things that made parts of it hang together.

The positive identification of Bill Crenshaw as "Cal" meant that Bill knew very well who the girl was who had shot Mac. He had lived with her, slept with her, traveled with her. Yet there hadn't been a word of identification from him to the police. Bill's involvement in the assassination of his brother was beyond any doubts. The testimony of Scatback and his disciples could finish Bill Crenshaw forever when the time came. Moss and Garth, the FBI people in Washington, would be fascinated to know that Arthur Austin, the dead agent, could have identified Bill as Caligula, the assassin's lover. Bill was done for, sooner or later, but like a wounded animal, his death struggle could be mortally dangerous. If it weren't for Maggie, they could have gone to the police with their evidence and wrapped him up.

But what about the Old Man? Was he in on it as Scatback thought? Or was Zachery here quite legitimately looking for the man behind the gun? Was Bill playing games with his own people or was Scatback right?

Cotter remembered a conversation he'd had with Senator Farraday long ago about multinational corporations. "Look at General Motors," the Senator had said. "Twenty-eight billion dollars in annual sales; Dutch Shell, twelve and a half billion, CrenAm God knows how much more. No government can regulate giants like that, certainly no democracy. They're like fat men who can't stop eating. The lobbies are too strong. Human life is far too cheap a commodity to stand in their way. There is no law to control them."

But would the Old Man go so far, his goals threatened, as to kill his favorite son? Cotter, huddled against the cold, thought bitterly that God Himself had allowed his only begotten son to be crucified. Human life, too cheap a commodity. Maggie could mean nothing to the Old Man but a source of information, critical to his problem. After that she was garbage, to be thrown on the town dump!

Cotter felt his whole body shaking.

He had no sense of time. The urgency for action was so great that every breath he took seemed to take forever. Actually something happened much sooner than he could have hoped

170

for if he had tried to predict. There was a faint scratching noise on the frosted side window of the Ferrari. At first he thought it was a roadside bush, blown by the wind. But then the noise turned to an urgent tapping.

Cotter reached into his belt and brought out the Police Special he was carrying. Then he leaned over and rolled down the window on the passenger side. It was too dark to distinguish a face, but a small unsteady voice asked: "David?"

"What's up?" Cotter asked.

"It's Patty," the voice said. "May I get in?"

"Of course." Cotter reached for the dash light button, but the blonde girl sensed or felt what he was doing.

"No lights!" she said. "The man at the gate."

Cotter leaned back against the leather seat. "Scatback sent you?" he asked.

"Who else?" The girl shivered. "God, it's cold!"

"Carl got to him?"

"How else would I have found you? Scat thinks you're right, David. We can't wait."

"To do what?" he asked bitterly.

"Country power lines are still rather primitive," she said. "A tree falls across the lines between poles and a whole section of the countryside is without power, in the dark. A tree is about to fall across the lines a little way down the road, David. It will take out not only power, which means lights, but also the telephone lines, which means the power failure can't be reported. There are about ten of us ready to go in."

"Without power the outside lights at the house will be gone," Cotter said, leaning forward. Time to go! Now!

"There'll be something inside the house," Patty said. "Country people are prepared for power failures. They happen often enough to be ready. Candles, maybe a flashlight or two. But it should be reasonably confused."

Cotter turned his head. She was there, but he couldn't see

171

her. "You're going in, Patty? You don't have to—for me—you know."

"Scat says go, so I go, David. But there are instructions. About nine of us and you are going in. The theory is to get to the house from all sides, attack from all sides at once. We're to time it. You see that light across the valley?"

He could see a single pinpoint of light shining in a distant window.

"When that goes out, we go. But not together, David. Each of us to approach from a different angle. I have two instructions for you. First, if someone starts beating up on you in the dark, say 'Scat!' good and loud. If it's a friend, he'll back off; if it's an enemy, fight for your life."

"And the second?" Cotter asked.

A mittened hand reached out and rested on his arm. "We have only one objective, David. It's to find your girl and get her out of there. If you hear anyone shouting 'Go! Go!' it means she's been found and someone is taking her out. There'll be two cars cruising out here on Route Twelve. If you hear 'Go!' get out of there fast, get back here to your car, and get to town. If you're not the one who finds her, just go. Scatback says you're not to delay to carve your initials into anyone. Just get out of there, leave on your own. We'll catch up with you later."

"It's got to work!" Cotter said.

The hand tightened on his arm. "Timber!" the girl said softly. "It's time."

Across the valley the eye of light had gone out and there was darkness.

"Good luck, David," the girl said, and she was quickly out of the car and gone.

For the first time in hours Cotter felt warm. Action and hope set his blood pounding. He found the trail he had made

172

going in and coming out a while back. It was easy this time. He could almost run toward the target. He was out in the clear before he knew it, partly because the house, daylight-bright the first time, wasn't even a shadow in the darkness. He paused, blowing on his hands, searching for bearings. And then he saw a sort of firefly blink of light ahead of him. Someone behind a window in the house was maneuvering a flashlight. Another tiny light flickered at a second-floor window. A candle.

He plowed through the knee-deep snow toward those tiny beacons. Off to the right somewhere he heard the sound of what he thought was some night bird. It was instantly answered somewhere to his left. Scatback's people, he realized. Through the darkness and across the snow they were all moving in.

One thing none of them had any way of guessing was how many people there were in the house. The ex-Senator lived there with servants, Hunter had said. How many and how tough they would be in a fight there was no way to know. Zachery was there, and he would be tough. He was a killer. Red Christie's blood might still be on his hands. Someone must be guarding Maggie if she was still there and alive. That wouldn't be left to amateurs, Cotter told himself. How many of the Old Man's army were inside?

Scatback's plan was obvious. They would all crash into the house at the same time, racing from room to room in a search for Maggie. In the darkness and confusion they could hope to find her, carry her off.

Cotter stumbled over something and felt an agonizing pain in his right leg. It was a garden bench, a stone bench, buried in the snow. For a moment he felt paralyzed. He thought his leg must be broken, but a moment or two later he was able to limp on toward the house.

He could hear voices now. Inside the house someone was shouting to say there were candles in the dining room. It was a voice Cotter didn't know, probably Martin Cleary's.

173

There was the sound of breaking glass and the voice from inside was louder. "For Christ sake, you don't have to smash up the joint to find a couple of lousy candles!"

Cotter guessed that one of Scatback's people had smashed a window to find a way in. He stumbled against a heavy pillar, and realized he was at the front portico. He had seen it well lighted a little while ago. The heavy front door was just ahead of him. He found it, fumbling in the darkness. The knob turned in his hand. Many people who live in the country don't lock their doors. He pushed it in and was greeted by warm air. He stepped inside and closed the door, standing with his back to it.

The darkness was total, but people were calling to each other.

"I have the candles, Mr. Cleary!"

"Well, for Christ sake, bring them into the living room!"

Off to the left Cotter saw a light flicker, and then the figure of a man carrying two lighted candles in silver candlesticks crossed the entrance hall beyond Cotter and went into an adjoining room. He hadn't bothered to look in the direction of the front door. The people in the house weren't aware yet that they were under attack.

And then the voice Cotter identified as a servant's voice, the man with the candles: "The telephone's out of order, too, Mr. Cleary. No way to notify the power company."

"Damn! Well, someone else will get to them. It must have knocked out the whole area."

"I don't like it," a strange voice said. "You're sure someone hasn't cut just your line, Cleary?"

"The whole valley is dark, sir," the servant said. "I could see that from the upstairs window."

"So we just sit here and wait?" the strange voice asked.

"Nothing else to do," Cleary's voice said. "Unless you want me to send someone into town. People closer in will report it before we can."

"I still don't like it," the strange voice said. "There's something screwy about it."

Then a third voice spoke and Cotter felt his heart jam against his ribs. He would know that harsh, rasping voice anywhere, he thought. It was Ross Crenshaw, the Old Man. "You got nerves, Zachery? No one's crashed the front gate, or the man out there would have reported. That's your own intercom system, isn't it, Cleary? Not connected with the power lines or the phone? So check with him."

Cleary evidently went into an adjoining room without coming out into the hall where Cotter crouched, unable to get moving. He could hear Cleary's voice in the distance, but not what he said. Then he rejoined Zachery and the Old Man.

"All quiet out there," he reported. "He confirms the fact that the whole valley is dark."

"All the same, I'm going to have a look around," Zachery said. "God damn it, I've got a feeling."

At that moment, from somewhere on an upper floor, a woman screamed. It was cut off abruptly. There was the sound of running feet. Zachery came charging out of the living room, flashlight in hand. He headed for the winding stairway, swearing. He hadn't turned his torch Cotter's way.

Cotter moved, running. The first thing Zachery would check on was Maggie—if she was still there. As he reached the foot of the stairs, Cotter came face to face with a white-haired man carrying a candle. The ex-Senator shouted at him: "Who the hell are you?" Cotter hit him squarely in the mouth and he went down, crying out as he fell. Cotter raced up the stairs after Zachery.

The second floor was suddenly a madhouse. People seemed to be running everywhere, opening and closing doors. Someone ran into Cotter, grabbed him, began choking him.

Cotter managed to gasp out "Scat!"

He was instantly released. The person who'd attacked him said: "She has to be on this floor. We've been through the one above. Goddamned maid screamed when we went into her room." It was the voice of Carl, the motorcyclist.

Blindman's buff! No candles here, no torches. Fumbling along the wall, Cotter found doors. He opened one into darkness.

"Maggie!"

Nothing.

He moved along to a second door, opened it, called her name, and nothing. He had drawn his gun and was carrying it at the ready. He opened a third door, and was instantly blinded.

Three powerful torches focused on his face. He couldn't see what was behind them. Someone shoved him forward and he heard the door slam shut behind him. The rooms must be soundproofed, because the noise in the hall was suddenly shut off.

"Stand quite still, Cotter," Zachery's voice said. "Don't think of shooting, because I'm holding the lady in front of me."

One of the torches moved and Cotter saw her, held back against someone, the coppery hair hanging down to her shoulders. His breath made a hissing sound between his teeth. She looked like an old woman.

"If there is some way you can get rid of these people in ten seconds, you won't have to watch me gouge out the lady's eyes."

"Please, David, for God sake shoot!" The words came from between Maggie's lips, but it was not her voice.

"Eight—seven—six—and drop the gun," Zachery said.

The sonofabitch meant it. He would do it. Cotter dropped the gun onto a thick rug. He turned for the door and opened it.

"Go!" he shouted at the top of his lungs. "Go! Go!"

A few voices shouted and people seemed to go running from everywhere. Cotter turned back into the room, once more in the beam of light from the three torches.

"That meant that I had found her, was taking her out," he said in a flat, exhausted voice.

"How too bad for both of you," Zachery said. "Because you must realize that neither one of you is going anywhere now."

"Unless you just enjoy killing for the sake of killing," Cotter said. "Those people you let me send away know that I'm here, that Maggie's here, and why. Their next stop is police headquarters. The ball game is over."

"The ball game has only just begun, Mr. Cotter," Zachery said. "Let's move!"

Cotter never knew what was meant by that last, because the man who had been behind him at the door leveled him with a savage blow from a gun butt.

Cotter opened his eyes. How much later it was or where he was, he had no idea. He was lying on his side, his knees drawn up in a painfully cramped position. He tried to straighten out his legs and found that he couldn't. He raised an arm and found it obstructed six inches above the top of his head.

He was aware of movement, of a humming sound he couldn't instantly identify. The pain in his head felt as though it had been split open with an ax. He tried shifting his cramped position again, without luck. Suddenly it dawned on him where he was. The trunk of a car! The humming sound was tires on a paved road. He managed to move his arm so that he could see the illuminated dial of his wristwatch. Two o'clock! It had been only a little after nine when he and Scatback's people had raided Martin Cleary's house. He must have been bouncing around in this coffinlike space for four or five hours. He reached up and touched the back of his head. Agony! He wondered if it wasn't something of a miracle to be alive at all.

He struggled a little to change his position. His whole body ached.

Rather slowly he began to put together the possibilities. Mac Crenshaw had called George Zachery the general of his father's army, a man who made split-second decisions and acted on them. He hadn't waited to find out whether Cotter's statement that people would be heading for the police was true. Cotter's unconscious body had been stuffed in a car trunk; Maggie could be riding above him in the same car. Five hours meant they could be two hundred and fifty miles from Brownsville by now. It would be no problem to average fifty miles an hour along no-traffic roads. To be taken where?

Cotter tried to imagine what could be happening in Brownsville. Scatback and his people, hearing the "Go!" signal, had rushed out of the house and headed for escape routes. The cruising cars on Route 12 would have picked most of them up. They must have guessed or known that the signal to leave had come from Cotter. Had some of them waited for him to appear at the red Ferrari, bringing Maggie with him? When he didn't appear, they must have thought he'd been forced to head out in a different direction. They would have drifted away, some back to Scatback's farmhouse, some into town to wait for Cotter to show.

How quickly, after Cotter failed to appear, would they act? Would they, as Cotter had assured Zachery, go to the police? If they did, would Captain Shane believe them? Even if Scatback expounded his whole theory of the crime, made his identification of Bill Crenshaw as the boyfriend of Marcia, the assassin, would he believe? Would Shane believe enough to go out to the Cleary place? And if he did, what would he find? An outraged Martin Cleary, declaring these hippie kids had broken into his house during the power failure, probably to steal whatever they could lay hands on. Frightened off by Cleary and a couple of armed servants. Cotter? Never heard of

178

him. Margaret Branson? Never heard of her. Of course, search the house. There would be no trace of anything to back up Scatback's story. But the red Ferrari, parked along Route 12, would prove Cotter had been there. But there would be no red Ferrari parked down the road. It would have been removed by Cleary's people or Zachery's people.

So Shane would have searched the house, at Cleary's urging, and found nothing. Cleary would make a formal charge against Scatback's army for breaking and entering. Oh, they would play it very cool. Bill Crenshaw would probably be found at the Brownsville Ski Club. Confronted by Scatback, who would identify him as Cal, or Caligula, Marcia's lover, Bill would have been highly amused. He was William Crenshaw, for God sake! Surely Shane wasn't going to take the word of these wild-eyed anarchists? It was well known that for years they'd been demonstrating against big corporations like CrenAm. Now they were trying a cheap frame-up. Was Shane crazy enough to believe that he could be involved in his own brother's murder?

All of this would have taken time, a couple of hours at least, while Cotter lay, unconscious, in the trunk of a car, miles away. Scatback wasn't going to be able to make it stick; not in the early going, at least; not in time. Scatback would probably find himself in a cell, along with some of his people, at the State Police barracks, on a charge of housebreaking.

And so, Cotter told himself, there would be no help. Not soon enough, at any rate. What was the phrase they'd used in the Watergate days? He and Maggie were going to be "deep-sixed."

Cotter's mouth felt dry. Maggie! He had only had that brief look at her in the light from Zachery's torch. He had only heard those few words spoken out of a twisted mouth in a strange voice. "Please, David, for God sake shoot!" He had understood it well enough. She couldn't stand any more, couldn't take any more, would rather die. It wasn't a decision he could have made in the tick of seconds. A man like Zachery might have. All the alternatives were at Zachery's fingertips all the time. He might have acted, had he been in Cotter's shoes. He might have known there was no future for either of them, have opened fire and killed his woman to save her further anguish and faced his own death, quick and clean. Cotter hadn't been equipped to take advantage of that moment. Now Maggie would have to face more, and he would die in a much messier fashion.

The car hummed along the road, mile after mile, minute after minute. The driver stuck at a fast, steady pace. They weren't hitting towns, Cotter thought. It had to be Thruway driving. Thruway to where and to what final end?

Cotter's dry lips moved and he spoke her name. "Maggie!" He had gotten her into this. He had failed her. "Please God, give me just one more chance."

The car rolled on. Cotter found himself slipping in and out of consciousness. Was it exhaustion, or was the damage to his head that bad? The drive seemed to go on forever.

And then it stopped. There was the slamming of the car's door. There were muffled voices. And then the door slammed again and the car moved again, creeping now in low gear. And then it stopped again. Doors opened and closed. More voices. And then there was the sound of a key in the lock of the car's trunk. The lid was lifted and Cotter was blinded by bright sunlight.

"He seems to have made it," a man said in a voice Cotter seemed to remember but couldn't place. "All right, buster, let's get you out of there."

A hand gripped Cotter's, and jerked him toward the opening. He almost screamed from the pain of sudden movement. He found himself falling out of the trunk and onto the ground.

"Upsy-daisy," the man said, and tried to pull him to his feet.

180

Cotter opened his eyes, still narrowed against the light, and recognized the man from the bookstore across the street from Maggie's apartment—the man with Arthur Austin's FBI credentials. "I figure you're not in shape to use the karate skills you mentioned the other night. Try walking. That'll be tough enough." He had a white smile that suggested he was enjoying himself.

Cotter's legs simply wouldn't hold him up for a few minutes. As blood began to circulate in those long cramped legs, the pain was unbearable. But finally he was able to take a couple of staggering steps, the bookstore man holding onto his arm.

The car had been driven into some kind of barn or shed that had high windows at the far end through which a bright morning sun poured light. Through one of the windows Cotter caught a glimpse of a building he remembered. They were at Mac Crenshaw's Virginia property.

The bookstore man dragged Cotter forward toward a door which he opened and Cotter was pushed through. He fell down onto his hands and knees. He was aware of the clean smell of saddle soap. They were in some kind of tack room, saddles on racks, bridles hanging from metal hooks, saddlecloths. In a far corner was a glass case protecting blue, yellow, and red ribbons, trophies from horse shows. There was something beautifully neat and clean about the place. Cotter wasn't interested in the room itself, but in the people who were there.

Zachery was sitting on the edge of a long stretcher table, his eyes narrowed against the smoke from a cigarette. The bookstore man, smiling and smiling, stood behind Cotter, blocking the door. At a far window, looking down over green fields, was the unmistakable figure of the Old Man, Ross Crenshaw. Lying face down on a pile of blankets against the far wall was what was left of Maggie. She didn't even turn her head to look at Cotter. One bare arm, thrown out from her body, had the dark marks of small burns on it. The cigarette torture that Scatback had mentioned. Oh, the bastards, the miserable bastards!

Cotter struggled up to go to her, and knew he couldn't make it without falling again.

Slowly the Old Man turned from the window. He was wearing the black glasses Cotter remembered.

"I warned you to stay out of this, Mr. Cotter," he said. "Unfortunately you weren't willing to take advice. And so, it seems, we come to some kind of payoff."

Cotter sucked air into his lungs. "A dead end for both of us," he said. "Too many people know the truth for you to make it."

"Just what is this 'truth' so many people know, Mr. Cotter?"

"That you planned the murder of your own son," Cotter said.

Not a muscle twitched in the Old Man's face. Zachery sat frowning at the red end of his cigarette.

"Proof?" the Old Man said.

"For free?" Cotter asked. "You're not going to let me testify, or Maggie testify, so why should I help you to silence other people?"

"The black man?"

"What black man?" Cotter said.

"There was always the risk he might recognize Bill," the Old Man said, like a man impersonally adding up a score. "But not very dangerous, Mr. Cotter. There was a wild phase of Bill's life. He was involved with that girl a year or so ago. But he reformed, came home, began to operate like a civilized man."

Cotter's hands were clenched at his sides. His eyes were on Maggie, lying motionless on the pile of blankets. "Would you describe your world as civilized, Crenshaw?"

"You're not a realist, Cotter," the Old Man said. "My world is the world of business. Business is being conducted now the way it's been conducted for most of this century. Modern politics support modern business. Yes, that's today's civilized way of life."

Cotter remembered Farraday's phrase and he quoted it. "Business as usual, politics as usual, murder as usual."

"The battle cry of today's liberal idiot," the Old Man said. "Too bad we don't have time to discuss the philosophy of today's way of life." The black glasses turned toward the motionless girl on the pile of blankets. "An extraordinary woman," he said. "Great courage. Too bad she can't use it in a sensible cause. I could use someone with her guts in my world." He sighed. "I have to break her down, you see."

"You've been trying to get her to tell you something she doesn't know," Cotter said.

"How do you know that?"

"Because I tried to get her to remember anything that might have someone after her. I didn't use your methods. She would have told me if there was anything."

"I'm afraid I can't buy that," the Old Man said. His black glasses glittered in the sunlight. "She was in love with Mac. Mac trusted her. I assume you've guessed that Mac had something on me, on CrenAm, on Martin Cleary and others who were involved. Mac held it against me, which is why, regrettably, he had to be removed. There are proofs of what he had, probably tapes, and he would certainly have turned them over to someone as insurance for himself. Who else but this woman, with whom he shared all his business and professional life, whom he trusted and cared for? There's no one else. I'm not afraid of your black man and his people, of his wild charges against Bill. That can be laughed out of court. But Mac's evidence I must have. I hope you'll persuade Miss Branson to turn it over to me."

"No way. She hasn't got what you want."

"I'm certain she has. Who else could Mac trust with something so sensitive? She wouldn't tell you, she wouldn't tell anyone. To tell would be violating a trust. That's the idealist's way of thinking. On the theory that every man has his price, we offered her a handsome sum of money. No dice. We then tried some of the simpler methods of persuasion, at which my man Zachery is an expert. You notice her arm, those little scars? Made by the hot end of a cigarette. There are others on other parts of her body. She wouldn't tell. Then came the somewhat more painful method of pulling out a few fingernails with a pair of pliers."

"Bastard!" Cotter heard himself whisper.

"We then turned loose several of Zachery's men to amuse themselves sexually with her. This is a method that has worked in the past with proud women, but not with her. They found her unresponsive."

"You filthy sonofabitch."

"Now we come to all that's left," the Old Man said. "Systematic mutilation. You will watch, and perhaps you will try to persuade her along the way that nothing, no loyalty, is worth what she will be subjected to."

Cotter lurched forward, out of control. Instantly a glittering handgun was aimed at him by Zachery. "I'll shatter both your kneecaps if you insist, Cotter," he said.

"I don't think mutilation is going to produce the results you want, Father." A woman's voice, cool, controlled.

Cotter turned and saw that Gwen Crenshaw had come through the door behind the bookstore man, who had been too occupied with Cotter's move to prevent it.

The Old Man's face was suddenly scarred by deep lines. "What the hell are you doing here, Gwen?"

She was wearing a loose-fitting tan polo coat. There was a deep purple scarf at her throat. Her skin was white, but that was its natural color. Dark hair hung loose at her shoulders.

"Looking for you, Father," she said. "Trying to save you the futility of trying to force people to tell you things they don't know. Did you think Maggie Branson was the only woman in the world Mac cared for?"

"Well, of course not," the Old Man said. Cotter sensed he was looking three moves ahead. "But when it came to business or professional matters—"

"Yes, we didn't have too much in common, did we?" She sauntered toward him as she talked. "But when it came to matters of life and death, I was his wife. He trusted me with his life."

"I don't follow you, Gwen. And I think—"

"Follow me," she said in her cool, level voice. "He gave me the evidence you're looking for, instructing me to turn it over to the special prosecutor if anything happened to him and I believed you were responsible. Well, I didn't believe you were responsible. I thought it was a political thing, another crazy crackpot of a woman. But Mr. Cotter made me think."

"Cotter?"

"He didn't trust you. It was obvious when he was here that day with Maggie. You didn't want her to leave, but he took her. And then his secretary phoned me to say that Maggie had been kidnaped. Who else could I think of but you, dear Father?"

The Old Man just stared at her through the black glasses.

"I chartered a plane for Brownsville and took the evidence with me to show to Mr. Cotter. He was gone, but there was wild talk in town, talk that opened my eyes, dear Father. So I took my chartered plane back to Washington and turned over what I had to Max Larkin, the special prosecutor."

"You stupid bitch!" the Old Man exploded. "If you'd given me a chance to explain—"

"I don't want explanations, dear Father. I want to square things for Mac. So, shall we keep all the murders in the family?"

She took her hand out of the pocket of the polo coat and shot the Old Man squarely between the eyes.

*   *   *

One of the strange things about wars is how the tide can change. Everything seems to go for one side, and then they extend themselves too far, make one tactical blunder, and the other side comes roaring in.

Half an hour ago, doubled up in the trunk of a car, Cotter had been certain of total defeat. Now, in something out of a wild nightmare, Ross Crenshaw, the master mind, the supreme planner of an evil conspiracy, lay dead on the floor of that tack room, Gwen standing over him, looking down at him as if she'd just crushed a poisonous spider under her heel. Zachery, of course, would now mow them all down.

But Zachery didn't. Zachery was the man, Cotter knew, who made split-second decisions. He made one now, which was to put as much distance as he could between himself and this holocaust. There was nothing he could do for the Old Man any more, and neither killing for the hell of it nor revenge was his game. Zachery took off, the bookstore man at his heels. Zachery wouldn't have dreamed that he had less than a minute to live when he ran out of that tack room.

The tide of the battle had changed. Captain Shane up in Brownsville had listened to Scatback's story, hadn't believed a word of it, and yet—and yet— He had telephoned FBI agent Wesley Moss in Washington. Bill Crenshaw had been the assassin girl's lover. There was a wild story that he and his father had arranged Mac Crenshaw's assassination. It was stated that Arthur Austin, Moss's friend and colleague, could have identified Bill Crenshaw as Cal, or Caligula. Moss and a car full of agents headed for Virginia. He thought it could be a starting point. It very nearly was the wrap-up point. Moss and his men were piling out of their car when Zachery and the bookstore man came running out of the tack room. When Zachery was ordered to stop, he opened fire, and both he and the bookstore man were mowed down.

In the tack room Cotter moved on his still wobbly legs to

186

the pile of blankets where Maggie lay. Her skin was clammy cold, her eyes closed. She was, he thought, in shock.

"Is there a telephone?" he asked.

Gwen, looking down at the man she'd killed, answered as though it was the most ordinary question in the world. "Just outside to the right of the door."

Cotter never got to the phone, because Agent Moss burst in, followed by a couple of his men. He stood gaping at what he saw.

"We need an ambulance," Cotter said.

"He's dead, for Christ sake!" Moss said.

"For Maggie!" Cotter said. The room was swimming around him. He took Moss by the shoulders and shook him. It seemed, somehow, the sensible thing to do.

It was late afternoon before the pieces finally fell into place. Cotter, near to normal as a result of optimistic news from the hospital, a shave, a steaming hot shower, and fresh clothes, was sitting in Max Larkin's office. The special prosecutor was tinkering with a tape recorder on his desk.

"Bill Crenshaw has been arrested in Brownsville," Larkin said. "For the moment he's charged with the murder of Arthur Austin, the FBI man. We need time to put together the assassination plot. With the Old Man dead and Zachery dead, it may be hard to prove. Cleary's in the jug for conspiracy to kidnap and torture Miss Branson. There's also a kidnaping charge against Bill, because he's the one who persuaded her to leave the Gateway Motel."

"How do you know?"

"She told me," Larkin said.

Cotter sat forward in his chair. "I was told she couldn't see anyone."

Larkin gave him a thin smile. "You're not the special prosecutor. Lots of guts, that girl. She's going to need a lot of caring for, though."

"She's going to get it," Cotter said.

"I hope she'll take it from you. She has a feeling that she's been spoiled, violated, made repulsive to you or anyone else who knows the story."

"What an idiot!" Cotter was on his feet.

"Sit down," Larkin said. "She was given sedatives after I talked to her. It'll be some time before she can talk to anyone." He glanced at a paper on his desk. "We think Zachery killed your man Christie. Zachery knew Christie had seen him talking to the bookstore man. All Christie had to do was mention Zachery's name to you and a can of peas would be opened. Proof?" Larkin shrugged. "Everyone involved is dead. We think Zachery also beat up your friend Jack Murphy in Brownsville—meant to kill him, but Murphy was too tough an old bastard to die. Murphy will settle that for us when he can talk. But of course the key to all this is here." Larkin reached out and touched the tape recorder. "It would take too long to play the whole thing, so let me fill you in." He leaned back in his chair. "There are countries in what we call the third world I never heard of. Mobardu is one of them. African. Black. Oil. Like most of these little countries, they started out to be free, democratic entities. Mobardu had free elections, but I suppose it didn't mean much because most of the people were too primitive to know what the hell it was all about. What they had was oil, quantities of it, and their friends, before freedom, were the Dutch. The newly elected President was prepared to deal with a Dutch oil combine. He believed what they promised him. But this didn't suit CrenAm. The Old Man wanted Mobardu's oil and wanted it badly. You and I know by now that people in high places in government are really errand boys for the big corporations. Senator Martin Cleary was an errand boy for Ross Crenshaw. The plan, as these tapes show, was to finance a revolution, provide it with money, arms, ammunition,

188

planes. Mobardu would fall into the hands of greedy terrorists to whom CrenAm promised the moon. Nothing new about this, Cotter, nothing strange. Business as usual."

"Murder as usual," Cotter said.

"An unlucky thing happened for CrenAm. Senator Cleary was picking up a fast buck everywhere he could. Unfortunately for him a brilliant young prosecutor in my office got on his trail."

"Mac Crenshaw?"

Larkin nodded. "He nailed Cleary but good. Not on anything to do with CrenAm, you understand. So Cleary, desperate, played the old American game of plea bargaining. He told Mac what was happening in Mobardu, how his father was involved. If Mac would let him plead to a lesser crime, he'd keep still about it. If Mac refused, he'd blow CrenAm sky-high.

"Now Mac had a weakness—his family. He loved the Old Man in spite of the fact that he was a pirate. Cleary was just an ugly piece in a grab bag of corruption. But Mac knew he had to stop the destruction of a country, of a free people struggling for a way of life. And so he went to his father. He played him a tape of Cleary's story. He was prepared to go easy on Cleary—no prosecution if he'd resign from the Senate. But his father had to forget about Mobardu. Mac would expose the whole thing if he didn't. Listen." Larkin switched on the tape recorder.

"That's final, Father." Mac's voice. "Pull out of this Mobardu conspiracy or I'll blow the whistle on you."

"I don't understand you, boy." The Old Man's harsh, rasping voice. "This isn't a new way of doing business. It's been this way all over the world, South America, the Middle East, Africa. Everywhere, God damn it. Big corporations live by bribes and helping the people who will help them get what they want. That's business, Marcus."

"Not for me, Father. Go ahead with it and face the music,

or forget about it and we'll both sleep better at night."

"Can't I make it clear to you, Marcus? What I'm doing is good for America. We have an energy shortage. This means millions of barrels of oil for America's needs. Who gives a good goddamn who runs that silly country?"

"They are a free people, entitled to operate the way they want."

"Oh, God, Marcus! Will you never be a realist?"

"It's an ultimatum, Father. You play it my way or else."

"You don't leave me any choice, do you?"

"None at all."

Larkin turned off the tape machine. "So Marcus Aurelius Crenshaw wrote his own death warrant," he said. "The Old Man could wait for the right time and the right place, and Bill dreamed up the fancy scheme that seemed unbeatable. There was only one thing wrong. The day after Mac Crenshaw was shot, the Old Man was handed a letter by someone. It was from Mac. Mac pointed out that if anything violent happened to him, an agent of his had tapes—the tapes of Cleary's confession, the tapes, in effect, of the Old Man's confession."

"The Old Man didn't know he was being taped?" Cotter asked.

"Obviously not."

Cotter's smile was bitter. "When the bad guys make secret tapes of conversations, we think it's criminal. When the good guys make them, we're grateful."

"We use what we can get in this business," Larkin said.

"What will happen to Gwen Crenshaw?" Cotter asked.

"She will become a very rich woman and, hopefully, make a better life for herself."

"No criminal charges?"

"The Old Man killed her husband, didn't he? And he was planning to kill you and Miss Branson, wasn't he? I think any jury would consider her a public benefactor."

* * *

190

Hours and hours later.

Cotter sat in a chair in a dimly lighted hospital room. Maggie, her hands bandaged, slept. Pliers had pulled out some fingernails. He could see the little spots on her arms, at her throat, made by Zachery's cigarettes.

She stirred, and Cotter sat straight up in his chair. "Maggie!" he whispered.

She opened her eyes and saw him. "Oh, my God," she said, and turned away.

He went quickly to her and put his hand against her cool cheek. She flinched as though he had hurt her.

"Please go away, David," she said, her voice shaken. "Don't you understand, it isn't possible any more for us after what—what they did to me? Please go away, David. It only makes it harder for you to be here."

"Would I go away from you if you'd been run over by a truck?" he asked.

"That's different, David. What matters is—"

"What matters is that I love you," Cotter said, "and nothing in the whole bloody world could turn me away from you. Like it or not, you're hooked, Maggie."

"David—!"

He put his arms around her and gently held her close. "In a day or two, when you're up to it, we'll go back to Brownsville, where I have a couple of people to thank. Jack Murphy and Scatback Hughes may just have kept us alive. After that, wherever you say, anywhere in the world, for as long as you say. I love you, Maggie."

She whispered his name, not too distinctly because she had slipped off into sleep again. But she was holding onto him as though her life depended on it.

NOW READ ON WITH KEYHOLE CRIME
Other titles available in the shops now

THE ROLLING HEADS
Aaron Marc Stein

When Matt Erridge stumbled across the breathtaking
Barbie on the beach at Dinard, she soon persuaded him
to take her round Brittany. But if she hadn't been so set
on going to Guimiliau, Matt might never have found her
dead in the bushes.

DEATH ON A BROOMSTICK
G. M. Wilson

Was Mrs Sibley, the elderly lady found dead with a
broomstick on the East Anglian marshes, really a witch?
Inspector Lovick joins forces with Mrs Sibley's landlady
to discover the truth . . . and finds he is dealing with an
evil far more terrifying than conventional witchcraft.

THE MENACE WITHIN   *Ursula Curtiss*

When she is left in charge of her aunt's house, Amanda
does not know of the secret underground shelter where a
murderer is hidden. But the murderer knows about
Amanda. And she has to be eliminated . . .

 Keyhole Crime